THE CLOVER TREE

Kimberly Foster

BALBOA.
PRESS

A DIVISION OF HAY HOUSE

ISBN: 978-1-4525-4778-7 (sc)
ISBN: 978-1-4525-4777-0 (e)

Library of Congress Control Number: 2012903502

Balboa Press books may be ordered through booksellers or by contacting:

Balboa Press
A Division of Hay House
1663 Liberty Drive
Bloomington, IN 47403
www.balboapress.com
1-(877) 407-4847

Because of the dynamic nature of the Internet, any web addresses or links contained in this book may have changed since publication and may no longer be valid. The views expressed in this work are solely those of the author and do not necessarily reflect the views of the publisher, and the publisher hereby disclaims any responsibility for them.

Any people depicted in stock imagery provided by Thinkstock are models, and such images are being used for illustrative purposes only.
Certain stock imagery © Thinkstock.

Back cover image and image of girl on front cover courtesy of
Lynette Johnson Photography, Seattle, WA.

Printed in the United States of America

Balboa Press rev. date: 3/30/2012

DEDICATION

To my parents who believed in making memories. And for Tim, Corinne and Katie who share my fondest ones.

ACKNOWLEDGEMENTS

Gratitude is the final piece in my journey. I offer overdue and sincere thanks to my varied and deep support system. To my family, friends and all whom I tapped your hidden talents thank you!

Without doubt my early readers were blessings: Jenn, Marie, Laura, Andrea, Lynda, Madelyn, Brooke, Lauren and my mom! Thankfully you laughed and cried and I heard your feedback-there is more "boyfriend stuff"!

The manuscript could still be collecting dust if not for the talent and competency of my editor, Meghan. And, to Kathleen and Sara, friends and coaches-one of whom nudged me to start and the other, to finishing!

Finally, I acknowledge my family to whom I'm most grateful. To my daughters, Corinne and Katie who eagerly kept asking, "How is your book coming?" And, while entering and navigating adolescence themselves, provided the real life fodder and voice for a young adult story. Lastly, to my husband Tim, who let the project unfold in its own time but never let me give up. All my love.

Part I

GRADE 7

CHAPTER ONE

As I emerge from my room on the first weekend of Christmas break, my late arrival to the family morning creates the reaction I expected, "Getting some beauty sleep?" my dad says. "Good morning Rip Van Winkle," my mom says in a coffee induced lilt. I've never asked her who the heck "Rip Van Winkle" is but she sounds sarcastic so I get the point. My sister Kelsey may or may not beat me to the breakfast table. She's only two years younger than me and having her own "growth spurts" so she can log some serious hours of sleep herself. But, I never wake up before my dad; and today is no exception. Just a few yards from my room, dad is already crunching numbers and staring at blueprints in our home office. It seems to me that being a perfectionist would be a difficult trait in the construction business. He is regularly complaining about project delays or inept contractors. A telltale sign that he is frustrated is when he starts yanking on his bushy eyebrows. You might think that he would be eyebrow-less at this point, but there are plenty left for him to tug on. I inherited the same eyebrows which have just recently become daunting. I turned 13 and now I have caterpillars above my eyes! My mom is no help. She draws in her eyebrows with a make-up pencil, so she thinks I'm lucky, but I don't like the unruliness of them. I stagger into the hallway, "Hey Dad." He's focused so I don't get a response. I turn toward the bathroom and catch a glimpse of my sister. There are no pleasantries.

"Hey, I didn't say you could use my straightener!" I shouted.

"You were asleep!" my sister barked back at me.

"So, you could have waited."

"No, I have Ellie's party and it starts soon. What's the big deal? I always use it."

"Not today."

"You are so mean!"

"Whatever."

"I hate when you say that!"

"Why do you have to straighten your hair anyway?" It bugs me that she has started grooming herself to look like me. I don't wait for an answer. "Put it down."

Kelsey shows some chutzpah, "No."

I lurch for it and inadvertently hit her in the face with my elbow.

In the usual progression, Kelsey lashes out at me, arms flailing and a few bouts of "I hate you Kate, I hate you!" These words tend to get my mom's attention and this morning, my dad's too.

"Girls, what's going on in there?" dad probes evenly.

But, my mom is already on the scene. "The bickering! You two can't even start winter break without fighting? I am not a referee!"

I roll my eyes at my sister and mouth tauntingly, "Dur, dur, dur."

My sister goes crazy. A possessed eleven year old is amusing. But my mom doesn't think so, and goes to comfort my sister. Kelsey is such a mama's girl; it's annoying.

Kelsey starts to explain through her tears, "Kate wouldn't let me use her straightener."

"Even though I told her no, she kept using it. So I grabbed it back," I quickly retort.

"And, hit me in the face!" Kelsey adds.

"And then she attacked me!" I embellish.

Mom interrupts, "I do not need the play by play. You know what to do."

She always makes us say sorry and hug each other. Sometimes we'll have to stay embraced while she goes on and on about how she spent her childhood praying for a brother or sister and how she just doesn't understand why we fight. Every now and then, she'll revisit it with me alone, "Sweetheart, your sister adores you. Why do you antagonize her?" And the truth is, because I'm thirteen and it is my personal responsibility to incite her. But, I usually just mumble something like, "Because she is annoying." Then mom marches off with some comment like, "I would have loved an annoying little sister, blah, blah, blah." However, today we aren't tortured for too long. While we are faking our hug mom says, "That's what I like to see, a little forgiveness."

There is no movement or response from the office. I wonder if my dad wishes he had a son.

I'm hovering in the doorway while my parents discuss my behavior in the other room. I can just picture the scene. Dad behind his desk, chair pushed back enough so he can cross his legs. Mom is standing on the other side of the desk talking at my dad while her hands do a little dance in front of her to emphasize each point of contention.

"Joe, I need you to intervene now and then. This teenage thing with Kate is everything I heard about. Our sweet little girl is becoming a distant memory and the teenage version is testing me at every turn!" It's possible her hands actually circled around to emphasize "turn".

"Alyson, what would you like me to do?"

"Get out of this office! You've been holed up this past year working while your little girl is growing up. For whatever reason, I cannot communicate with her right now. I need your help and Kate needs your stability."

I'm thinking that she is totally overreacting but whatever, the ball's in my dad's court now. His silence toward my mom's attack seems to represent the path of least resistance. And then, he can't help himself, "This office is my only reprieve from the estrogen that permeates this house." He has caught her by surprise.

"Are you talking about Kate?" she asks.

"I'm just saying… I've been waiting for this shoe to drop for 13 years; my daughter and wife with raging hormones simultaneously." I think I hear a smile in his voice.

Mom hasn't gone completely sideways because I hear her chuckle at his observation. "Well good. Another reason you can take the teenager under your wing," mom insists.

"Any suggestions?"

"Nope. All this estrogen has clouded my judgment. You are on your own. Let's start now. I'm going to get started in the yard where my plants can't talk back. Can you take Kelsey to her party?" mom asks.

I'm waiting to hear his reply and potential solution for my egregious behavior when my phone starts vibrating on my dresser. A text comes through. An invitation I can't resist.

"SURE. BE RIGHT THERE," I text back.

Pausing in my doorway, I realize their conversation is over. I didn't hear the outcome but knowing my dad, he will "ponder" it for a while. No knee-jerk reactions from Joe Malone.

"Hey Dad?"

"Yes?"

"Can I go to the athletic club?"

"Ah, I guess. What's going on?"

"Oh, Madi and …." I decide to keep it simple. "Oh, Madi just texted me; she's there and wants me to join her."

"Okay, but did you run it by your mom?"

"No."

"Well, you should. You know how it bothers her when you make plans without checking in." Between my mom and my sister, there's a lot of coddling going on. "K."

"And, when she says you are free, I'll run you over to the club."

I use dad's distraction to my advantage. "I could walk," I offer.

He doesn't even look up. "Just run it by your mom."

With a smirk and perfectly straight hair, Kelsey hops in the car next to dad.

"Hey Kate, I can give you a ride."

"I'm good walking."

"No really, get in. I'd like to spend a few minutes with you." Oh, great. He hardly had any time to ponder the grand solution to fix my behavior but it appears as though his intervention starts now. But, with Kelsey in the car, I'm spared for awhile; that is if playing car games sounds fun.

Kelsey suggests we play "Sweet or Sour" on the drive to Ellie's.

"That is so babyish!" I blurt out, "After all I am so much more mature."

"So what? It's funny! Dad, you'll play won't you?" Kelsey asks.

"Absolutely!" dad says. "Let's find out how many drivers are feeling sweet or sour today."

They start waving and hooting and hollering out the car windows. They try to get the attention of the other drivers and passengers. A smile or wave back means they are "sweet", a scowl means they are feeling "sour" today. Basically, dad and Kelsey are totally making fools of themselves. It's not enough for me to slouch down in the back seat.

"Stop it! You guys are so embarrassing! If I agree to play 'Slug Bug' will you *pleeeese* stop that game?" I beg.

"Sure! I love Slug Bug!" Kelsey agrees.

Dad spots the first VW and yells, "Slug Bug! I'm on the board with two points." And so it goes; a current model VW bug: two points, the harder to find, original, VW beetle: 3 points, and any

VW van: 4 points. Luckily it is a fairly short drive to Ellie's. Kelsey pulls off a last minute win as we pull into Ellie's neighborhood. Three Slug Bugs in front of one house? Hope they got a good deal.

Kelsey rattles off, "Slug bug, slug bug, slug bug!" before dad and I even notice them.

"Good win Kelse. Have fun at the party," dad says as she jumps out of the car.

"Thanks Dad. Bye Kate!" She has obviously moved on from the straightener incident.

"Bye." She does look cute. Thank goodness she has me to teach her a few things.

"Where have you been?" Madi anxiously asks. "The appointment is in 10 minutes!"

"I know, I know, my dad needed to 'connect' with me and started rambling on. I don't even know what I agreed to do with him!" I explain.

"We're gonna need to run. The tattoo parlor is four blocks away," Madi exclaims.

Within blocks of Neiman Marcus and Urban Outfitters, we see the tattoo parlor is snuggled beneath a piano store.

"What the heck? How'd you know about this place?" I ask.

"I didn't. Devyn posted the address when she told everyone about her appointment."

The green lights on the sign flashing TATTOOS guide us toward the shop. I expected a crowd gathered. After all, what 7th grader gets a tattoo? Madi and I slow down to catch our breath and assess the situation. Just across the street is the Starbucks my mom frequents and being in the heart of the city, it is likely I'd see someone I know. Walking into a tattoo parlor is not the info I need getting back to my already paranoid parents.

"Should we go in?" Madi asks.

"I don't know. Let's get closer." I say.

The green lights converge in on us. It's clear where we are headed. A small sign to the left of the door reads, SOULFUL SKIN. If they didn't have the flashing tattoo sign, I could've mistaken it for a massage place or something.

"Let's look in the window," Madi suggests.

"Okay. "

I'm surprised by the ambiance. It looks like an upscale nail salon; Persian rugs, comfy chairs, a small waterfall in the corner. And there she is, holding court. Her ladies in waiting surround her in deference.

"Who are all those girls?" Madi wonders out loud.

"I recognize Carly and Joanna. A few of them look older, huh?"

Front and center is Devyn. She is dipped back in a chair with her arm out. The artist is working on her upper arm.

My face is closer to the window and fogging it up. "Madi, no way! She is really doing it. Devyn is getting a tattoo!"

"Should we go in?" Madi asks.

"I don't know. I feel weird. I hardly know her."

"She posted it on Facebook. She wanted everyone to know so she could have an audience," Madi reminded me.

And then, I am so embarrassed to be peering in from the outside. Here we are, lured to the tattoo parlor so we could watch Devyn brand her body. She tosses her hair back and forth while the image continues to appear on her upper arm. She glances over toward the door and the glass we are peering through and gestures for us to come in. I tentatively open the door, looking over my shoulder while Madi checks her phone.

"Hi girls!" Devyn calls out to us. "Just in the neighborhood?"

"Ah, kinda," I say.

"Well, too bad you weren't here earlier to help me pick out the design. I went with a Monarch Butterfly. Isn't it awesome?" Devyn asks.

Looking at the orange and black wings I think to myself that it's not the prettiest butterfly I've ever seen and most importantly, it would be hard to conceal. However, I decide to keep this initial reaction to myself.

"Sure. Yeah, it's cool," I say.

Madi is speechless and keeps looking at the time. I'm glancing around the shop. There are books of designs and an entire area devoted to piercings. A guy with double digit piercings works on a client. Madi mumbles to me, "Let's go. My mom is picking me up at the club soon."

As our spokesperson I say, "Well, we need to go. See you at school in a few weeks."

"Sure. Bye!" Devyn says with enthusiasm.

We barely get out and around the corner when Madi starts texting like a fanatic.

"What are you doing?"

"Telling the crew about Devyn's tattoo; I want to break the news!"

"Damage control." It's all I can say to Madi who is in the eye of the storm. The wall posts are appearing lightning quick and it occurs to Madi and me that we cannot do anything about it. Morgan arrived for moral support.

"Ugh." Madi falls back onto my bed with the weight of our teenage world on her shoulders.

"The picture; I guess you can tell that it's us?" I ask. It's a statement and question at the same time.

"Thank goodness it was cold outside and our breath steamed up the window a bit. It really could be argued that it isn't us," Madi suggests.

"Yeah, in a court of law but not on Facebook; she's tagged us and everything."

"I never should have sent out that group text," Madi says.

"Well, who knew it wasn't a real tattoo? She played it up like it was."

"Still, I shouldn't have said anything. Devyn is ruthless."

"No kidding. Calling us Pollyanna's and voyeurs and, what else did she call us?"

"Peeping Toms," Madi reminded me.

"Yeah, right, just great; how can we be Pollyanna's *and* Peeping Toms?"

"Kate, this isn't the time to be logical. Do we answer back?"

"Oh, I don't think so." I think of my dad who rarely has a knee-jerk reaction and it seems to work out for him. "So, we look stupid for a day or two, it'll blow over. She'll find another way to get attention," I insist.

"Well, thank goodness we don't have school until January. I would probably have to transfer," Madi says, half joking.

"Okay, now you're getting dramatic. Don't lower yourself to Devyn the Drama Queen's level," I tell her.

"Easy for you to say; you're just an accomplice."

"What's up with the Monarch Butterfly anyway?" Morgan pipes up.

"I dunno. It was ugly for a butterfly" I say.

"She should have chosen a bee for 'Queen Bee'," Madi offers bitterly.

Morgan swipes her phone and bursts out laughing, "No way, get this…."

"What?" we say in tandem.

"I Googled 'Monarch Butterfly' and guess what it says?"

"What?" we say with urgency.

"It basically says that the Monarch Butterfly essentially has no brain! Its brain is microscopic. And guess what else? As creatures they are repelled by humans!"

This time Madi falls back onto the bed laughing and I belly laugh my summary, "So, Devyn's tattoo is a brainless creature that doesn't like humans? How fitting!"

CHAPTER TWO

"Dad, you've kidnapped me against my will you know."

"I would have added a blindfold but I can see that your eyes are hardly open as it is," dad replies.

"Yeah, it's a bit early. Don't ya think?" I ask.

"I needed to have you in a bit of a comatose so you couldn't resist."

"Ha ha. Where are we headed anyway?"

"You'll see," dad smirks.

"Well I know it's too early to be going to that Irish pub you make us go to,"

"Oh darn it. Wish I would've thought of that," dad says, pretending to be serious.

"At least I could've slept in."

"Maybe we'll hit it on the way home," dad jokes.

"Please, no! All that weird food like oysters and lamb and soda bread—yuck!"

"It's your heritage, Katherine Mary Malone. You must learn to like it." He's kidding – I hope.

"Dad, remember a few years ago when we were all in Seattle and you made us go there? It was a sunny day and you marched us into that dark, windowless pub!"

"Yes, it was wonderful," he states with confidence as if the passage of time changed the outcome.

"It was gross,"

"But that's when I met the owner and we've been friends ever since. He's on my St. Patrick's day list," dad reminds me.

And it comes rushing back to me and I start laughing, "Oh yeah, he called us 'lovely lassies' in an authentic Irish accent and then you introduced us in the same kind of accent, 'This is Katherine Mary Malone and Kelsey Colleen Malone' like saying our full names makes them sound more Irish or something." I'm totally making fun of him.

Dad's blue eyes become playful as I mock him. "Hey, hey...," dad warns.

I continue, "But then, you get to mom and just say, 'This is my wife, Alyson.' It was so awkward!"

"I don't remember any of that. I'm sure it didn't happen that way," he insists.

"Oh yes it did. I have cataloged every time you and mom have seriously embarrassed me. Believe me, I know."

"I'm sure you do," he says still smiling.

"Here's the pay off for getting up early." Dad pulls off the freeway and into the first driveway.

"Maple bars! Sweet!"

"We are early enough to get them fresh out of the oven," dad announces.

"Gooey and melty," I say.

"Yep. Just how we like them," dad confirms.

"Now I know where we are going."

"Some traditions never go away," dad says, looking at me lovingly.

"It's been a while," I admit.

All of the sudden I feel like I'm ten years old again. My entire pretense of being a disagreeable teenager slips away and I'm daddy's little girl. As my drowsy state starts to lift, an early memory of one of our first pilgrimages emerges. I drop my head back into the seat, close my eyes and I remember.

Maybe I'm ten or so and like today, I'm sitting next to my dad in the cab of his truck. I know his company builds things like stores and office buildings but I am not quite sure what he specifically does when he goes to work. When I've asked him about it in the past, he suggested I join him some time to check things out.

"Did we have to get up so early?"

"Mom wants us home later to help clean out the garage and I want to run by a job site and the office today," dad replies.

"Are the workers there?"

"No, not today, it is the weekend."

"Oh, bummer. How long at the job site then? It sounds boring."

"Not long. I just need to make sure my guys finished the drywall like they said."

"Couldn't you just call?" I ask.

"Sometimes I just like to double check. Besides, you can look for job site treasures while I kick around."

"Like what?"

"You'll know if you've found a treasure. Surprise me!" dad says.

Dad surprises me first with a stop at the donut shop. The maple bars are dad's favorite, so of course, they are my favorite too. We arrive early enough that the maple frosting is still melting. We pile back in the truck with our half eaten donuts and black coffee for dad, juice for me.

"Kate, check this out." Dad is sounding like a jokester. I glance over to see him moving his index finger up and down the side of his nose. From the viewpoint of the other drivers, it looks like he is picking his nose! Dad cracks himself up and I notice that the lady next to us is giggling. Dad notices too and slaps his leg in amusement.

We pull up to the job site and dad furrows his brow, bracing himself for whatever hiccup the project might present. He enters the front door, even though there isn't an actual door. I start meandering around the site.

I find a quarter and a decomposing Fanta can but that's it; nothing that qualifies as a "treasure". "Hey Dad, you done yet?"

"Almost honey. It's looking good around here—for once."

"Good. I wanna go," I say.

I can hardly wait to see my dad's office. He takes our school photos and Father's Day gifts with him every year "to his office" but where do they reside? Often his days are long and dad is rushing in the door for dinner so he definitely spends a lot of time at the office. I am about to get a visual on dad's second home.

His desk is large but sits in the middle of the office. The only extra chair has a pile of file folders on it so I nestle under the desk and lean up against a leg. Before I know it, my dad's efforts on the calculator have the adding machine tape running over the side of the desk and into my lap! As he works out the numbers and details of his project, I grab the paper and draft the most elaborate story a ten-year old can tell. I hand over my tale with great anticipation.

"Very clever story Kate! And, resourceful to use the adding machine tape! We will start a collection." Dad takes the story and tightly rolls it up. He secures the roll with a small paper clip and puts it in his desk drawer.

"Ready to head home?" dad asks.

"Yep! But, do I have to help clean the garage?"

He smiles, "We'll see."

Before we leave, I scan the office, taking in all the décor. Framed photos of our family, a rock sculpture I gave him for Father's Day, piles of paper and stacks of files. It's my dad's sanctuary. I love that he shared it with me today.

A sugar rush from the maple icing makes me more alert but I'm still not in the mood to roam around aimlessly. "Are we going to a job site?" I ask.

"Nope, just a quick trip to the office; I think the Office Manager filled up the snack machine," dad says. I'm being bribed, for sure.

The desk stands proudly in the middle of the office, just like always. Decorated by multiple file folders, a computer and the classic adding machine; it's the symbol of dad's work ethic and tidiness. Not a pencil out of place.

Even though I've grown a lot over the past summer I can still fit, so I find my spot under the desk and start writing. But this time it isn't stories; instead, I begin a list of my hopes and dreams. Now, it could have been a list of the boys I like, but that would have been too risky, so I went with hopes and dreams.

The calculator stops and dad peers over the desk, "Honey, I'm just about finished here. What's the story of the day?"

I pause and reply, "No story today. Just lists." Dad wasn't about to let tradition dissolve without inquiry.

"Lists? Anything you want to share?" he asks.

The voice of a newly empowered teen chimed in, "No."

He replies without pause, "What?"

"I just started writing down some hopes and dreams for myself," I explained.

When dad is amused, his blue eyes crinkle right before a smile appears. I recognize the look as he stands up and says, "Katherine, bring your list and follow me. I want to show you something."

As we walk outside, dad gives me some history, "When I was attempting to buy this office building there were other people interested in it. However, the owner of the building had a unique request. He was adamant that the new owner maintain a clover field that flourished on the property. I was the only prospective owner that agreed to preserve the field so he accepted my bid to buy the building. All I knew was that the previous owner considered the clover field magical. For me, a proud Irishman, I was delighted to preserve a field full of lucky charms!"

"For real?" I mused.

"Follow me. You can decide for yourself."

We came upon the clover field just past the covered area where the lunch tables are. It's far enough away that no one probably ever noticed it. As I approach the field, shivers run up and down my body. I look around and realize that this is not a random sampling of clover growing within a patch of grass. This is a pure clover field; clover upon clover. And, the delicacy of their leaves is not lost in the fact that they sturdily flourish season after season as one united patch. I lower myself to the ground and look at the clovers. The three pronged, heart shaped leaves do seem to emanate a certain magic.

Dad crouches at the edge of the field and says, "Choose a clover."

"One?" I ask.

"Just one," he confirms.

"They all look the same to me."

"But, they aren't. Take a deep breath and let your heart guide you," dad says.

Strange advice but I'm intrigued. I close my eyes and take a deep breath and guide my hand across a section of clovers. I open my eyes and pick one. I hold it in my hand and look at my dad quizzically asking, "Okay, like, what does this do?"

"Kate, pull out your list. I do not need to see it but choose one of your wishes. Assign that wish to your clover. Your clover represents something you want for yourself; anything." He continues, "It could be something tangible, like a new bike. Or something like meeting a new friend or getting a good grade. This clover field has no limits to granting your wishes."

I scan my list. "Okay, done." I really want to make the Premier soccer team and tryouts are coming up.

"Alright, so here is the deal. For this clover to truly manifest your wish, you must turn your desire over to the clover and consider it done. In your mind, your wish has come true."

I interrupt him, "I'm totally confused."

"Yeah, okay, I bet," dad says, "I glossed over the important details! Let's start over." "So, first label the clover. Label it with your wish."

In my head I say, "Kate makes the Premier soccer team."

"Then, visualize yourself with the wish coming true," he adds.

I begin. The vision starts with tryouts. I am wearing my Italia jersey since it is bright blue. I snuff out the idea of the Sounders jersey. I want to be unique. So, I walk on the pitch and we stretch and immediately go into wind sprints. I rock. I am *soooo* fast. The rest of the tryout is a breeze. I juke, I pass, I impress; and then, I see myself answering our phone at home to hear my new coach offering me a spot on the team. Dad continues his instruction while I work furiously to keep the image in my head.

"Now, give the wish feelings. How do you feel now that it has come true? What are your emotions?" I envision jumping up and down with the phone in my hand. I am so excited to have made the team. I whoop and holler and run around the living room high five-ing my family.

"Okay, so you feel the feeling; that's good. I see the smile on your face. It must be a great wish!" "Next, use all of your senses: does it evoke a taste or physical sensation? What do you see or smell?" dad asks.

All of a sudden, the image is no longer just in my head. I can feel the weight of the phone in my hand. I can smell the spaghetti simmering and my mom glancing over at me with anticipation. I can feel my excitement throughout my body causing me to bounce up and down like a kangaroo. I can hear my voice accept the offer in short, choppy sentences as I'm just too excited to organize my thoughts. I am the writer, director and actress of my own movie.

Dad waits a bit and then interrupts the movie with a final instruction by saying, "Next, consider it done. What does your life look like now that your wish has come true?"

I think to myself that it looks like this: I am walking onto the soccer field in my Premier jersey full of pride and anticipation. My teammates and I are all jazzed up to start our first game. Mom, dad and Kelsey are on the sidelines with coffee and hot cocoa smiling and eager to watch me play! I am psyched!

The final part of the ritual is next. Dad says, "Take the clover and thank it for granting your wish. Turn your wish over to the clover and move on with your life as if the wish has already occurred. If you start to doubt the clover, create the image again until you feel the feeling." He continues, "The magic resides in the feeling attached to the thought; otherwise it is just a wish that may or may not come true." I look around the vast clover field and feel a bit indulgent; a field ready to grant wish after wish? What a lucky girl to have such a smart dad to buy an office building with a magical clover field!

When we get home, I take my clover up to my room and tape it on to the wall next to my bed. I am so excited about my wish coming true that I decide to go practice some soccer on my own. "Mom, dad, I am going to the school to practice a bit."

My mom asks, "Can you take your sister too?"

"Sure!" Without doubt, this shocks my mother but I'm in a great mood.

"Hey, Kelse! You wanna go to the school and kick the ball around?" If my little sister is surprised by my generosity, she doesn't show it.

"Sure, Kate!" she responds.

"Grab some cones," I tell her.

"Okay!"

Tryouts are in a few months but I prance around like a US National Team member. In the meantime I decide to make some additional wishes that can give me more immediate gratification. Before I know it my single PREMIER SOCCER TEAM clover is joined by the *A* ON MY MATH FINAL clover, the NEW PAIR OF JEANS clover and the EATING LUNCH AT THE COOL GIRLS TABLE clover. All of these wishes are starting to get confusing, so I pull them off my wall and paste them on a large poster board. I label them so I can really visualize each one. The cluster looks like the top of a tree, so I add a trunk and deem it my "Magical Clover Tree". There is a lot of room for more clovers. My hopes and dreams will be the fertilizer to make the tree grow and grow!

My clover ally will surely pull through but I'm really nervous about the Math final. Right before the break, I tanked a quiz and my teacher claimed that it's my nerves that derail me, not that I don't understand the material. Oh great, how do I get around that? I'd rather not understand it; at least I could get help with the material. So I spent every night before winter break ended visualizing my clover tree wish. Plus, I studied and studied and studied, just to be safe. Armed with the real sense that I achieved an "*A*" I marched into class with confidence.

I wasn't surprised when the test came back in my favor. My first clover tree success! Thank you bountiful clover tree!

The jeans wish is a good challenge since Christmas just passed. But, a girl can never have too many cute jeans so I imagine myself stuffing my jeans into my tall Uggs, walking out the front door and plopping down on the bus. It wasn't for me to question the ultimate source of my new jeans since it didn't matter; they were already mine in my visualization. But, when I arrive home a few weeks later and there is a pair of True Religion jeans on my bed, I almost faint. I feel like I am in the presence of something larger than myself. Where did they come from? I haven't told anyone about my wish. My mom is outside mowing the lawn, so I tip-toe out of my room toward the back door wondering if I might catch a glimpse of the fairy that deposited my new jeans on my bed.

"Mom, where did those new jeans come from?" I ask tentatively.

"Oh, yes, try them on. Susan gave them to me today. She found them at the Rack. They were too big for Morgan and they were such a good deal she thought they might work for you."

"Right, great – okay, thanks." And then I remembered the

gratitude element of this whole manifestation process…, "Thanks clover tree!" I shout.

With my belief in the clover tree firmly intact, I confidently march over to the cool girls table the next day wearing my cute new jeans, of course. I convince Morgan to join me. After all, we know a lot of them from elementary school and the few new faces, while very pretty and groomed, look very nice. There are rumors, but I haven't actually ever witnessed anyone being turned away. But today, I am confident. I see my friend Madi at one end of the long cafeteria table.

"Hi Madi." And without asking, I forge my way in between Madi and her friend.

"Hey Kate."

"You remember Morgan, right?" I ask.

"Yeah, of course," Madi says as Morgan finds a spot at the table.

Madi offers, "This is Lucy. She went to Medina."

"Hi Lucy," we say.

Thankfully, we blend right into the conversation. They talk about the same stuff we talk about. Today we are comparing notes about Mr. Metcalf, the Social Studies teacher who goes off topic on a daily basis.

Madi says, "Today he overheard that Matt went to Costa Rica and rambled on about how educated the 'Ticos' are; that's what he called them. And how beautiful the country is and how yummy the food is for like, 40 minutes!" She continues, "It's not like any of us will be heading to Costa Rica anytime soon, ya know!"

Lucy jumps in, "At least it has something to do with Social Studies. During our class he starts talking about autism and we kept asking random questions to see how long we could keep him off topic! It is like a game."

Morgan ventures into the conversation, "I have him too and our class is so naughty! A few of the boys ask him the same question every day just to see if he notices. So far he hasn't!" You go girl for jumping in the conversation! I pinch myself over our good fortune. Any doubts I secretly harbored about the clovers are quickly dissolving. They are magical and I can have whatever I want! Do I dare tell Morgan how this happened? No. I will let her think our charming personalities and cute jeans earned us a spot with the popular girls. I smile broadly and bite into my lunch. Cool table entry was seamless!

Lunchtime affords a whole new dynamic. Morgan and I become regulars at the "cool" girls table. Occasionally some boys mix in; apparently, "boyfriends" of some of the girls but you would never know it. The girls treat them horribly so I'm not sure why they endure it. But, not for me to decide as they didn't even know my name. Then, I look toward Devyn at the other end of the table and she is holding court. Boys and girls gravitate to her every word. She is the diva. our grade. She seems to hold the social strata in her hand so I try to play by the rules. I am a small fish in a big pond.

At our end of the table, Carly's upcoming sleepover is the hot topic. I guess I will have a chance to figure out Devyn's allure this weekend since Carly invited her too. Apparently, Devyn gets invited to everything. I'm still not sure if that's because she's fun or if it is some sort of unwritten diva rule. Again, I'll find out soon enough. Curiosity aside, I am feeling pretty good about getting an invite. I really want to be accepted; and, I have an idea.

CHAPTER THREE

With the sleepover in mind, I asked dad for a handful of clovers earlier in the week. He obliged without questioning my motives. I am glad about that because, while my intentions are good, I am about to pass along some privileged information.

"I need a ride to Carly's house," I say.

"I need a ride, please," dad says, reminding me of my manners.

"I need a ride pretty please, awesome Daddy," embellishing my request.

"*Please* will be fine. I will take you," he says.

"Okay, cool. Let's go."

On the ride, dad informs me that he will walk me up to the door to meet her parents.

"But mom already spoke to them on the phone," I insist.

"I know, but I like to double check these things. You know, give them the 'up and down'." He thinks he's funny.

"Okay, but keep it quick, alright?"

"Will do," dad says.

Mr. and Mrs. Bryant are passing dad's inspection so I scoot on in to join the girls. I yell over my shoulder, "Bye Dad, love you," and run upstairs. I am the last to arrive, so I inventory my options and take the sleeping spot on the end next to Morgan.

The sleeping bags are side by side in their enormous bonus room. Everyone has their own pillow with their favorite pillowcase on it. Thankfully my cute polka dot one was clean.

With our camp properly organized we head outside before dinner. One of Carly's neighbors is a cute boy named Ryan. He and some buddies are skateboarding up and down the street. It is hard to look casual, six giggling girls, but we manage to drum up a reason to be outside. So before we know it we are walking around the block trying to look busy. Devyn decides we should go chat with the boys but all of us are just fine with our "looking busy" program. "You guys are so lame," Devyn proclaims.

"Devyn, it's not that. We have to get back for dinner," Carly says. Ingenious!

We rush through dinner so we can get back outside. The boys are gone so we remorsefully head back inside to chill. Despite the disappointment, everyone gets along great and the mood starts to get silly. Devyn whips out some mascara and shows us how she can put it on perfectly without a mirror. Admittedly, I am impressed. I haven't received the official make-up A-Okay at my house yet, so that does seem like a legitimate skill to me. With her dark, Cleopatra features, she doesn't even need mascara. Then, Joanna takes her right hand and makes a fist. Palm facing us so the fingers were lined up in a row like piano keys. And then, her thumb, which was in the normal position perpendicular to the fingers, turns and aligns itself with the row of fingers! So, we were staring at a row of four fingers and an inverted thumb! There are shrieks of amazement and exclamations as we yell, "So creepy!" She giggles, delighted to freak us out with her double-jointed thumb! And so it goes, everyone presents a trick, skill or story to contribute; a sleepover rite of passage. I purposely wait to go last because I know I have a really cool thing to introduce.

The girls are perched, ready to hear my news. I pull out the clovers. The small bouquet pinched between my fingers clearly needs some explanation.

"What have you got there, Kate?" Carly asks.

"Magic clovers," I reply.

"What?" the girls ask in unison.

"Yeah, these clovers will grant your wishes. I've gotten a new pair of jeans and an *A* in Math and…," I pause to catch myself from blurting out, "a spot at your table at lunch". Instead, I simply add, "… and other stuff too."

"You just make a wish?" asks Morgan, who probably can't believe I haven't told her already.

"There's a little bit more to it than that," I continue, "Here, each of you choose a clover. The best part is yet to come!"

There's mild interest but mostly blank stares. Remarkably, my enthusiasm does not wane as the girls reach in and select a clover.

Before I can continue with all the important steps for creating the wish, I experience the "Devyn factor". She doesn't even offer slight skepticism. Instead Devyn says with conviction, "Kate, you are so stupid; everyone knows it HAS to be a four leaf clover to mean anything." The first thought that runs through my mind: "Oh, I am so wishing I would have just shown them how fast I can finish a Rubik's cube!"And then, the disproportionate weight Devyn's opinion holds is enough to break the watershed of naysayers.

Carly says, "That's like, really weird. Why do you need a clover? I just ask my parents for what I want."

Lucy says, "My parents tell me to ask God for what I want."

Leah says, "I just don't get it." Madi looks at me longingly but stays silent.

My best friend Morgan says, "I think it is worth a try," and I love her for that.

Morgan's brave act of loyalty does not diminish my humiliation. I feel my face turning bright red and I want to crawl into my sleeping bag and disappear. And, the thought of my sleeping bag makes me think I better sleep with one eye open tonight. Devyn may concoct some way to draw clovers all over my face if I don't watch out. My mind is racing as I try to salvage the situation.

Unwittingly, Devyn spares me with a change of subject and says, "I wonder if we could get away with 'rolling' Ryan's house tonight?" Mostly nervous laughter is the united answer.

Leah asks, "Carly, do you think we could sneak out later tonight?"

"We'll have to figure out other ways to get in trouble. My mom is one step ahead of us. She promised me all our toilet paper has been inventoried and accounted for and is under strict surveillance."

Wow, Carly is a master. She knows how to diffuse Devyn every time. I better take notes.

We stay out of trouble which suits me just fine. I can't help but be preoccupied over my misstep with the clovers. While it appears the clovers have been dropped and dismissed, I feel my popularity is also on the verge of being dropped and dismissed. I am so confused. Something I believe in with conviction was questioned. I need to talk to my dad.

The next day, I can't get home fast enough but dad isn't home from Kelsey's game yet. I try to wait patiently but the afternoon is dragging along. "Mom, where is dad? Shouldn't they be home already?" I inquire.

"I asked him to stop by the sports store and get her some new running shoes. But, he mentioned stopping by his office, or something. And, you know Kelsey, I'm sure she sweet talked him into a yummy lunch somewhere too."

"Oh, okay," I say with a hint of discontent in my voice.

"Anything I can do?" Mom offers, sensing my disappointment.

"No, I'm good. I have some homework. I'll be back in my room," I reply.

"Alright sweetie; let me know if I can help."

Hours later, they arrive home. Kelsey has a bag full of stuff. She swindled dad out of more than just running shoes. She starts to show me her loot. "Dad got me some new Under Armour and this water bottle I've been wanting for—ever." She turns "forever" into two words for a dramatic effect. Kelsey goes on,

"I picked out one for you too. You will love it. My friend Sophie has one and I used it once, and it is the best water bottle!"

I've never heard anyone get so excited about a water bottle. But, that's Kelsey. It's hard to curb her enthusiasm. Before I know it, mom is calling us for dinner and I've yet to sort out my dilemma. At the dinner table, mom and dad bring out the usual line of questioning after a sleepover and I answer: "Yes, so and so was there. Yep, so was she. Nope, she had relatives in town. Yes, I got enough sleep. We had hamburgers. Yes, I was polite. Yes, I tried to eat everything. No, nothing out of the ordinary happened." (I lied).

Dinner and dishes completed, I head to my room to prepare for the upcoming school week: finish homework, organize my backpack, and choose my outfit. Kelsey calls me "anal", I call it "organized". !

I hear my dad enter the office and sit down at his desk. This is a common Sunday evening event. He likes to prepare for the week ahead too. I walk in and sit down on the floor. I spill the beans about the failed clover presentation and sigh, "They'll rag on me forever about this."

Dad turns his desk chair to the side so he can see all of me. He swipes at his unruly brows and begins. "Honey, I'm sorry that happened to you but I hope you can see the gift in all of this."

I think to myself, geez, why does he have to be so philosophical all the time? I just want him to tell me that the girls were wrong, I was right, and that it's possible that I can still sit at the cool table at lunch.

He continues, "What do you think the silver lining is?"

I ponder the question. I seriously pondered it because I had already thought about it all weekend and didn't come up with any "gifts" just some plans for self-salvation. "Well, the gift would be that no one ever talks about it and it is totally forgotten like as if I never even brought up those stupid clovers."

He chuckles. "Well, that would help you in the short term but I was thinking about something else. I want you to remember how you felt when your belief was questioned. What were you feeling at the time?"

"I wanted to run and hide. Reverse time. My stomach sank and I felt judged."

"It made you feel vulnerable, right?" dad asked.

"Yes," I confirmed.

"Honey, this is the deal. It is okay to be excited about something new in your life. And, it feels natural to want to share it with the world. But, the lesson is to really make sure you share your most personal secrets in a safe environment or not at all. Also, ask yourself, what is the purpose of sharing; an altruistic motive or a personal one?"

Dad and his big words; "What is altruistic?" I ask.

"It means selfless giving. Were you selflessly sharing the secret of the clover so your friends could get what they wanted? Or...," he paused, "was there another motive?"

I couldn't lie. "It was both. I truly wanted my friends to have the gift of the clover but I did expect that it would help me be accepted in the new group. Now, I feel so dumb and mad that I exposed the clover."

"Well, it's done and you've learned a lot about who to trust and what to share with outsiders. I also hope you realize that you sure don't need a magic clover to have friends. Do you want to borrow my St. Patrick's Day cap to wear to school tomorrow? It has a lot of clovers on it!" He says chuckling and crinkling his eyes.

"Ha ha. Night Dad, love you. And, thanks."

CHAPTER FOUR

As I enter 4th period Science class, I scan the room for Morgan. She isn't in her seat. Lunch is next and I need some moral support before I sit down with the sleepover crew. After my talk with my dad, I decided I wouldn't "self ostracize" myself; I'd let the whole clover thing blow over. You know, lick my wounds and turn the page, so to speak. I am praying the topic won't come up at all. What are the chances? The distraction at the sleepover helped, but I know just one comment in jest or malice could make me the center of attention. And, the kind of attention I *don't* want. The bell rings and no Morgan. While I am lowering myself into my seat, I remember that she had an orthodontist appointment and will miss lunch too! I am flying solo.

Mr. Benson is a funny Science teacher. He really likes his job and he makes class interesting for us. Everything was clipping along and I really did forget about the impending lunch hour. Mr. Benson starts talking about blood and how some people can't stop bleeding when they have a wound and then, you have to use a tourniquet which makes your hand turn purple… and before I know it, Campbell from a few seats away turns green over the topic and starts throwing up. It was so spontaneous he doesn't have time to put it anywhere but the top of his desk! The whole class is in awe over the spectacle and thank goodness Morgan is at her appointment because she would have been in harms way! Mr. Benson is frozen as Campbell tries to evacuate but he can't get to the sink in time. It is so disgusting! Campbell's desk mate is so nice; he starts wiping up the mess. There is no way I could have done that without going into heaving fits myself. Finally, Mr. Benson gets his act together and sends Campbell to the nurse. My goodness, you'd think a Science teacher could handle some vomit but, not that guy. Basically, we spend the rest of class recovering from Campbell's weak stomach and I am having a "yay for me" party in my head. I feel bad for Campbell and his misfortune, but I was just bailed out. I have a story to tell to fill up the lunch hour.

My bailout plan doesn't turn out to be necessary. Before I even sit down, the entire 7th grade is talking about poor Campbell, funny Mr. Benson and how Science was cut short for the day. It is perfect. All anyone wanted to know from us eyewitnesses was the color of the vomit. That seems to be the most interesting part. After some discussion, we suspect he must have had a smoothie or something colorful for breakfast, because it looked like a rainbow snow cone coming out.

I enjoy repeating the events from Science class throughout the day. I tell my sister and she is jealous. She proclaims that the coolest things happen in Junior High! I share it with mom while she is cooking dinner. She laughs. She is most amazed that we could talk about it while eating lunch. Good point. I pass it on to dad before I go to bed and the first thing he asks is, "What color was it?"

Just when I think the clover thing had blown over, I'm thrown a curveball. I enter the locker bay for the quick turnaround off the bus and to 1st period. Junior high tradition is to celebrate friends on their birthday by decorating their locker. I'm immediately confused when I glance up from the distance and see a colorful display on the front of my locker. My birthday isn't until the Fall. Instinctively I feel uneasy. And, sure enough, I should. Any confidence I exuded when I innocently entered the locker bay deflates at the words, CLOVER GIRL BELIEVES IN LEPRECAUNS TOO! and WISH ON A CLOVER FOR A HAPPY DAY!. Shamrocks litter the front of my locker. Surprise, surprise; the author is unknown. Morgan, who arrived just seconds before me isn't sure who made it either. The bell is about to ring, but time is stopped as I stare at the poster. As only a best friend can do, Morgan swiftly grabs the corner of the poster and rolls it up. She shoves it in her backpack, "I wouldn't want the artist to fish it out of the garbage and try again." It's early enough in the day so there's probably not too much damage but the mean spiritedness of the gesture lingers. "Thanks Morgan. Those frickin clovers aren't feeling very magical after all." Morgan laughs and pats my back. We walk out of the locker bay side by side. The bell rings, but we don't change our pace. I take a deep breath and brace myself for the day.

I alternate between sad and mad all morning. Way to wreck my day, whoever you are! Mom even packed an extra yummy lunch and now I'm not even hungry. But, I'm not going to let the mystery person see me upset. Got it? I walk to the lunchroom and pause before the entrance. A few deep breaths will help.

With resolve, I walk confidently to the lunch table. And I surprise myself. "Thanks for the poster. It's not even my birthday so what a surprise." I pause. "No one signed it so I'm not exactly sure who to thank." My voice is steady and monotone. Carly starts chewing on her fingernails, Abbey looks down at her food, Joanna starts wiggling her weird thumb. No one makes eye contact except Devyn.

"Oh, that's right, I saw something colorful on your locker this morning. Are you having a great day?" Devyn's sarcasm is not lost on me or anyone else. Yet today I learn that a subtle reaction is a great tool. I muster up a response with feigned confidence, "The best day ever." Morgan nudges me under the table in support.

Madi smiles broadly which buoys me too. I may have successfully diffused the prank but I'm quite aware that not everyone at this table is a friend. But on this notable day in Junior High, I am beginning to unearth my real friends and real self confidence.

I march straight home still wounded from the poster incident. I walk in the house and holler, "I'm home" to no response. I instinctively walk outside to the back porch and spot my mom in the garden. "Hi Mom! I'm home."

My mom is an artist. Her garden is her creation and her solitude. This is the place where she finds her soul. How do I know this? It's not difficult to see her spirit soar while she prunes the Camellia or deadheads the Rhody. She touches each leaf like it is a gift from the heavens. She admires each flower and bush and delivers it to its perfect spot in the yard. It is obvious in the peaceful expression on her face. Dad pointed this out to me once and I cannot help but notice it when I find her in the garden. Dad works a lot and the reality is that she spends most of her time tending to us. Her time in the yard is the fragments of free time she carves out for herself.

She responds, "Hi sweetheart. How was school today?"

"Fine," I mutter.

"Okay. I'll be back here by the Roses if you need me."

"Okay," I say. And then, I decide I have more to talk about today, "Mom?"

"Yes?"

"Who is your best friend?" I say this from the top deck so she doesn't get the full impact of the question.

I walk down the steps and look at my mother with her gardening gloves on and her hair pulled back with too many of my hair clips. Her outfit is a combination of old workout clothes and dad's sweatshirt. She is begging for an extreme makeover. She starts to quiz me. I tell her about the issues at school.

"Oh, Mom. I kinda embarrassed myself at the sleepover at Carly's and someone made fun of me today about it on a poster. It was taped to the front of my locker when I arrived at school today!"

"Oh sweetie. That's terrible!"."

"I know," I say as my eyes well up with tears. I start to cry. Mom pulls off her gardening gloves and drops them on the ground. She wraps her arms around me. I am sobbing. All of the emotion I kept under control at school gushes out.

"Do you have any idea who did this?" mom asks.

"Well, probably someone from the sleepover. Not Morgan of course. But she doesn't know who did it either." The crying subsides. "Madi and Morgan were good friends though. They were really supportive at lunch and Morgan took it down right away. I was paralyzed but she shoved it in her backpack.

Good to have a friend that's quick on her feet!" she tries to add some levity for a second and then adds, "But, that's pretty mean Kate. How'd the rest of the day go?"

"I put on a good front at lunch. Hopefully the culprit didn't get the response she wanted."

"I'm proud of you sweetie. Way to bounce back. Let's hope taking the high road pays off." She's looking at me straight in the eye sending me all her motherly love and compassion. It helps.

"Hope so. Thanks mom."

"No problem. Keep me in the loop, okay? I don't want this to get out of control."

"I'll be fine."

"I know you will. We all have to survive Jr. High." She's serious, like she's remembering something but I just giggle at the idea that my mom was ever thirteen. She comes back to the present and continues , "weren't you starting to ask me something when you walked down here?"

"Oh yeah, I was wondering who your best friend is?" She considers the question briefly and I suspect she knew the answer the whole time.

She replies, "Well, you know I have several girl friends that I consider very important to me like Susan and Michelle. But truth be told, your dad is probably my best friend. What that means to me is that he sees my warts and all and still loves me."

I had heard the "warts and all" cliché before so I knew what it meant.

Mom continues, "Not all friends have that loyalty. But Kate, let me tell you my secret; my hope for myself is that someday, I will be my own 'Best Friend'."

"What does that mean?" I'm frustrated because she's talking in circles.

"It means that I hope to love myself someday as much as I love you, Kelsey and daddy. I'm working on it. And when I am in the garden, I feel creative, confident and free. I know it is hard to understand but if you could learn these lessons early, your life will be more free and conscious," mom *tries* to explain.

This so wasn't helping me with the poster issue. But, maybe it was. All I could paste together is that my mother is content. Warts and all she finds her place of peace. That is what I want.

Carly is nervously waiting for my bus to arrive. I see her fidgeting by the bike racks as soon as the bus turns onto campus. Madi and I scramble off the bus because there is barely enough time to get to our lockers before the bell. I don't know what Carly's issue is but I head toward the locker bay. She slides up beside me and whispers, "Can I talk to you for a sec?"

My stomach lurches a bit as I wonder what is going on. "Ok. What's up?"

"Well, I really have to tell you something and I feel really bad about it," Carly says.

Now I really have an uneasy feeling and if she doesn't get talking I will be late again to 1st period. "What?"

"It's about your locker yesterday," she starts tentatively.

"Yeaaah?" My curiosity peeks.

"Well …," she stammers, "I did it." And then the floodgates open and she is talking super fast in an effort to spit out the details before I can process her confession. "Devyn made me. She told me she would tell Ty that I liked him and that I have photos of him all over my room, which isn't even true and that I've never kissed a boy and I want him to be my first kiss."

"Wow," is all I can say.

"I know; she is so mean. And I really didn't want her to talk to Ty and tell him those lies so I went ahead and made fun of you. I didn't have a choice," she rationalizes.

"I guess not." I'm not inclined to agree or disagree at this point but I appease her.

"I'm so sorry. Are we still friends?" she asks.

The impending bell nagging at me, the confession, the betrayal and all I can say is, "Yeah, sure."

"Oh good! See you at lunch!" And off she goes, officially forgiven.

Devyn doesn't know I know about the poster. I'll be a better friend to Carly than she was to me, and keep her secret. After all, Devyn just wants a reaction. The lunch table conversation moves on to more important issues like, the next sleepover or latest cell phone app anyway. But, as my dad would say regarding the poster incident, "What's the gift?" My first impulse and answer to him would be to give Devyn the gift of ringing her scrawny neck. But mean spiritedness aside, the real "gift" is to consider my alliances. Would I second guess her motives in the future? Absolutely. But today, I am too distracted. Premier soccer tryouts are tomorrow!

CHAPTER FIVE

My feelings on the eve of soccer tryouts are a mixture of nerves and excitement. It seems not long ago that tryouts were months away and now as I lay in my bed, my mind bounces back and forth between confidence and doubt. I know that the coaches look for speed and ball skills so I perfected some "moves" so they would come naturally. But, I wonder if they will notice my understanding of field position and my sharp, crisp passes? Tryouts are a sea of talented soccer players; will I stand out? I stop myself. My mind is running amok. Then I think, Kate remember, you already gave up this dream to the clover tree. I rein myself in and quickly recall all the carefree months when the dream no longer resided in my mind. I need to go back there and trust the power of what I already created. I turn on my bedside lamp and look at the clover labeled, PREMIER SOCCER PLAYER and assure myself through all my senses that what I want is coming.

It is too bad that I have to endure an entire day of school before tryouts. A handful of girls from school are also trying out this evening and the ripple effect of their nerves is starting to get to me. At lunch every possible outcome is considered and the girls are working themselves into frenzied states: "What if all but one of us makes it?" and "What if they want girls that have played together before?" Or, "Do you think it matters that I only played Rec soccer up until now?" And on and on and on!

I survive the school day with my confidence in tact only to encounter my mother who is barely keeping her own nerves in check. On the way to tryouts she asks me over and over again,

"Kate, how are you doing? Are you nervous?"

"No, Mom, I'm not nervous."

"Kate, do you feel prepared?"

"Yes, Mom, I feel prepared."

"Kate, just do your best, it will all work out."

"I know Mom."

"Kate, remember, hustle out there. They look for a good attitude too you know."

"Mom! Stop it! All these questions are making me nervous!"

"Oh, oh, I'm sorry sweetie. You'll do great. I'm not going to watch though, okay?"

"Geez, Mom, you're killin' me."

I really wanted to choose my tryout number but they just handed me a penny with "61" on it. Neither six nor one is a favorite number of mine but this isn't the time to worry about luck. I drum up all the confidence I began the day with and jog on out to the field.

The coaches said that they would post the results online the following day but I had heard that they called each player first to get their commitment. So, with the prospect of a phone call, I insist that we go straight home after the tryout. Mom found a calmer version of herself by the time she picked me up and agrees to make dinner instead of grabbing food on the way home. Dad calls from work to find out how the tryout went. His line of questioning is as irritating as my mom's.

"How do you think you played?" dad starts.

"I played well," I responded.

"Did you play with the girls you met at the Premier clinic?"

"Yep, they were on my field."

"Good, good. Did you run lines? Show them how fast you are?"

"Yeah, we did some running."

"Were you the fastest?"

"I was one of the fastest."

"Were the coaches taking notes?"

"Yep."

"Did they ask you your name?"

"Nope. But they asked me how many years I've been playing and where."

"What did you say?" dad asks.

"I told them how long I've been playing." Didn't I just tell him that?

"Did you mention the camps and clinics?"

"No, Dad." I'm annoyed.

"Why not?"

"I didn't think of it."

"Oh well, it probably doesn't matter; just as long as you were playing on the top field."

"Dad, we'll find out soon, okay?"

"Oh, I know. I'm just excited for you."

And I think, or are you excited for you? Parents are crazy. They manage households, negotiate contracts, stay calm during trips to the ER, but when they can't control a particular situation with their kids they really unravel.

I'm finishing my homework at the kitchen table. I want to be as close to the home phone as possible. It's impossible to concentrate as I wait for tryout results. Math is the worst choice as my mind darts. Then, finally, the phone rings! "Check the caller ID, check the caller ID," I holler!

My mom says, "It's an unknown caller!" I better grab it. I jump up but let my mom answer it.

As I reflect back, it is eerie how similar the outcome is to how I envisioned it. Mom wasn't making spaghetti; instead, enchiladas.

But, everything else, including me jumping up and down like a kangaroo was the same!

Dinner became a celebratory meal. And, as we raise our glasses to toast me making the soccer team, dad says, "The Irish are at their best when there is something to celebrate! Congratulations Kate. Your hard work paid off! Cheers!"

After dinner and dishes, I race to the computer to check the overall tryout results. There is my number "61" near the bottom of the list. It looks like they are in numerical order. For all the right reasons, they don't list the names, only the tryout number. I close my eyes and concentrate, trying to remember everyone's number. I look for Madi's number, #24. Sweet! She made it. I glance at the list. I recognize a few numbers as girls who played on the top field with me. Otherwise, it appears as though I will be meeting a lot of new people. As I'm scouring the website for more information, an IM comes in from Madi: MY MOM WOULDN'T LET ME CALL. SHE THOUGHT IT WAS TOO LATE AND TOO "PRESUMPTUOUS" YA KNOW, BUT I SAW YOUR NUMBER ON THE LIST! HIGH FIVE!

I write back, YEAH, YOU TOO. IT'S GOOD TO BE GR8! I WONDER WHO ELSE MADE IT. DID YOU RECOGNIZE ANY OTHER NUMBERS?

KIND OF, BUT NOT REALLY, Madi responds.

I type, YEAH, ME 2.

GOTTA GO FINISH MY HOMEWORK BUT I'M 2 PSYCHED 2 CONCENTRATE! Madi types back.

I KNOW, ME 2. OK, WELL, CU TOMORROW!

K, BYE, Madi signs off.

Madi and I are giddy with excitement but we are walking on eggshells not knowing the outcome for everyone else. A few girls ask us at lunch if the results are up yet. We immediately know that they probably didn't make it if they didn't receive a phone call so we downplay our answer.

"Yeah, the tryout results are posted on the website by tryout number," I say.

"Did you make it?" Stacy asks.

With mild enthusiasm I respond, "Yeah, we both did."

"Oh, that's great!" she says more enthusiastically than I may have in her position.

Stacy continues, "Did you notice if #33 was on the list?"

Luckily I can answer honestly, "No, I didn't notice. But, I really only knew mine and Madi's numbers. That's all I was looking for."

"Yeah, okay. Hey, I might run over to the computer lab and try to check before lunch ends. Bye!"

Ooooh, I wish she wouldn't do that. If the news is bad, does she really want to be at school when she finds out? My own excitement is tempered by Stacy's very likely disappointment.

I skip tutorial so I can get home and find out who else made the team. Hurrying off the bus I get a text from Madi, "RESULTS R IN! R U HOME YET?" I'm jogging and texting simultaneously which is hard to do. "NO, ALMOST. CALL U IN 5." Dropping my bags, I plop down on the couch to call Madi. The back sliding door is cracked open so my mom must be in the backyard gardening. I better tell her I'm home first. "Hey Mom! I'm home!"

"Hi Kate! How was school?"

"Fine!" and I head back towards the couch. But darn, she wants to talk.

"Kate, the Premier soccer roster came through on my email if you are interested." I'm not really listening carefully so I don't hear all the detail. I'm dialing Madi instead.

"Madi, what's up?" I ask.

"Our team roster, silly!" She is gregarious. Madi rattles off some names, none of which I recognize nor does she until near the end, "Sara Blake".

"That sounds familiar for some reason," I interject.

"Yeah, for me too," Madi agrees.

But we aren't too worried about how we know the name because we will find out soon. Madi says, "Here at the bottom of the email is a notice about our team meeting. Tomorrow night! Already? That rocks!" We discuss how we *must* go together since we don't know anyone else.

My parents agree to drive separately so I can ride with Madi. We both decide to wear our cutest jeans, Toms® shoes and some layered tees. In just the past few days this common activity is forging a better friendship between the two of us. As we enter the host house I notice that some girls have already hopped onto the trampoline in the backyard, and a few look nervous on the periphery. It is comforting to have a wing "man" in Madi. My parents arrive shortly behind us and are immediately accosted by someone calling themselves the "Team Manager". They are handed pieces of paper and name badges. Mom and dad are smiling willingly at the manager. They might be just as excited as I am about all of this.

Madi and I mill around the food table and grab some chips. We see our coach mingling with some parents. The dad he is talking to looks really intense and Coach looks uncomfortable.

I overhear the dad say, "I will buy all the practice jerseys. Don't you worry about it!" He obviously wants everyone to hear him, because he is loud. And then, the man slaps Coach on the arm. My parents will die at my hands if they embarrass me like that. I'm fairly confident they won't, but ever since I made the team, they have been strutting around pretty proudly themselves; like they did anything! Weird.

Madi and I are done at the chip station but don't know what to do. Then, at nearly the same time our eyes land on a familiar face. That's Sara Blake! We nudge each other and in unison say, "The girl from L.A. class!"

"Let's go say hi," I urge.

Our duo is now a trio.

CHAPTER SEVEN

Who knew, Sara and I were just lunch tables away all this time! Thanks to soccer, Sara is becoming a good friend and an awesome tablemate at lunch. She always has something interesting to report. And, Sara has a great vocabulary which makes her stories all the more captivating. In fact, sometimes she sounds just like an adult. If I were to say, "Spanish is torture now that I have to sit next to Ethan," she would say, "The extent to which a class is enjoyable largely depends on who sits next to you". And thus, during this day at lunch, she told her story of Enrique and Spanish class. We all sort out our lunches and there's a pause before conversation breaks out.

Sara says, "My Spanish teacher re-arranged the seating assignments today and now I sit next to a troublesome student named Enrique."

"Is that his real name?" Madi asks.

Sara clarifies, "No, Enrique is his Spanish name."

"What does he look like? Is his name Ethan?" Morgan inquires.

I interrupt, "Morgan, there are like, 800 kids at our school. How is she going to know if it's Ethan?" Then I asked a more pressing question, "What do you mean by troublesome?"

Talking with Sara always offers some vocabulary lessons. "Oh, he is constantly on the verge of detention. His name is always on the board due to his outbursts in class. It is a challenge for him to sit still and listen," Sara explains.

Morgan mumbles, "I bet it is Ethan."

Sara continues, "So, when I had the opportunity, I asked Enrique, 'Why don't you enjoy this class?' And he scoffed at me and said, 'Because I have to sit next to people like you.' "

"Omigosh, like, what did you do?" asks Madi.

"Well I was taken aback by his response and considered what he meant by it. I think he just feels frustrated that he always sits next to students that listen and enjoy the class. I wasn't offended." And then her face lit up and she became a 7th grader again adding, "And then, the funniest thing happened! Our teacher, Senora Bennett came by with her puppet, Pepe. Enrique gets agitated and exclaims, 'Enrique is not here. Enrique is invisible to Pepe!' " Sara starts to giggle.

We join her giggling and that is just the start of it. Sara continues to explain that her Spanish teacher uses a puppet to help teach the language.

Sara adds, "Senora Bennett keeps the doll in a box and talks to the puppet in Spanish. She pulls it out of the box to mimic Spanish dialogue with it. We all think it sounds creepy."

And then we are all laughing so hard when Sara describes how the teacher walks around the class and has the puppet give the students hugs! We all agree that, despite his generally poor behavior, Enrique is smart to avoid that creepy puppet!

CHAPTER EIGHT

Adverse weather is not adverse if you don't know any better. Until today, it didn't occur to me that playing soccer in heavy rain, sleet or even snow was unusual. Living in the Pacific Northwest means you do most activities in the rain and you gear up and play. My mom calls us, "tough chicks" for getting out there in all types of weather.

Dinner and dishes done, I'm playing games on the computer when I receive an email from my new teammate, Janie. She is a really good soccer player who just moved up from Southern California. They play a different brand of soccer down there. She has awesome foot skills and speed, so she has been a great addition to our squad. However, when she missed practice tonight, I decided to shoot her an email.

The reply was simple but not anything I had ever considered, "HEY KATE. SOCCER PRACTICE? YOU MEAN IT WASN'T CANCELLED?"

I instant messaged her back, "NOPE."

"THAT'S WEIRD. MY MOM SAID IT WAS CANCELLED BECAUSE IT WAS RAINING SO HARD."

"SAY WHAT?" I reply instantly.

"YEAH, IN SOCAL WE DON'T PLAY IN THE RAIN BECAUSE IT WRECKS THE GRASS FIELDS," she responds.

I reply, "LOL! WE WOULD NEVER PLAY SOCCER IF THE PRACTICES AND GAMES WERE CANCELLED BECAUSE OF RAIN!"

Janie replies, "OMG, MY MOM IS SOOOOO CRAZY! I BET SHE EVEN EMAILED THE COACH. HOW EMBARRASSING! DO YOU THINK THEY WILL KICK ME OFF?"

I quickly respond, "OF COURSE NOT! BUT, KNOWING COACH TOM YOU'LL GET A REALLY NICE NICKNAME LIKE, "LITTLE MISS SUNSHINE!"

"DON'T GIVE HIM ANY IDEAS!" She begs through cyberspace.

"I WON'T HAVE TO. AFTER I THREW UP AFTER A GAME, HE CALLED ME "PUKEY MALONE" FOR MONTHS! GOOD LUCK! HA HA."

Janie signs off, "GOTTA GO KILL MY MOM. JK. C U."

"K. NITE." I giggle and decide that I'll never look at a Californian the same again! Tough chicks prevail in the Northwest!

CHAPTER NINE

I'm thinking to myself, I will never forget this drive as long as I live! We are driving to Walla Walla for our first road trip soccer game. Mom and dad are up front. Kelsey stayed home with a friend, thank goodness. She always wants to hang out with me and my friends. When my mom makes me include her it is so annoying because she acts even younger than she is. She'll try to tell stories from school like, "Hey guys guess what. Today at school we made silly putty in Science class. Mine's neon green. Wanna see it?" Like we really want to hear about 5th grade; if she was here she'd be humming some annoying tune incessantly because she knows that bugs me. Or, she would ask all my friends to play car games with her like "Slug Bug" and they might join her just to be nice even though they wouldn't want to. So it was cool of my mom to make arrangements for her so I could enjoy the road trip even more.

Mom and dad are letting us listen to my IPod on a speaker in the back seat which is also pretty cool. I'm sure they can barely hold a conversation as it is so loud. Anyway, I've got Madi, Sara and Janie riding with me. We are blasting our tunes and singing along. Mom suggests that we "try to sing and not yell" but we think we *are* singing already.

It's like a caravan. Our teammates are divided amongst a few other cars. The parents are doing a good job staying together. We stopped at one rest stop and apparently we all took too long. Abbey tried to get a cup of coffee from the nice people offering free coffee but they told her she was too young. And the bathrooms were so smelly that we all had to wait outside for our turn to pee. Mrs. Liu spent the whole time brushing out bits of potato chips from the backseat. My mom joked with her that there was more of that to come but she insisted that they wouldn't get to eat in the car anymore; bummer for them. But, the end result is that there are no more stops until we arrive at the field. We don't care. Even though everyone is texting furiously amongst each other, we have still managed to make some signs to hold up in the windows. Some are messages to our friends: ABBEY, YOU ROCK! Others are for the neighboring drivers to see: HONK IF YOU LOVE SOCCER! We get a few responses. Who doesn't love soccer?

The five hours fly by for us. I look up front and my mom is trying to flip through a magazine but since she keeps glancing back, I figure the reading isn't working out for her. Every now and then she reminds us to drink some water to stay hydrated. Dad seems content driving and being alone with his thoughts. Or eavesdropping, I suppose.

Just as Taylor Swift's "Love Story" comes on, dad announces, "Five minutes!"

A rousing "Sweet!" from all of us and we proceed to drown out Taylor Swift with our rendition of the song:

"That you were Romeo, you were throwing pebbles
And my daddy said stay away from Juliet
And I was crying on the staircase
Begging you please don't go and I said,
Romeo, take me somewhere we can be alone,
I'll be waiting all there's left to do is run
You'll be the prince and I'll be the PRINCESS (we yell that really loud)
It's a love story baby just say YES (that is really loud too).

We won the game—thank goodness. It was a long enough drive home as it was and mom and dad have to replay the whole game. Five hours is a lot more time than the usual 20 minutes it takes from our home field. I'm willing my teammates to keep their answers short and simple. I can only hope this will discourage my parents from pressing on about the game.

"What did Coach Tom say after the game?" Mom asks.

"I don't know. That we played well."

"You did! Was he specific?"

"No. Just that we may win our league if we keep playing like that." Oh, too long of a response. I opened up my dad's favorite topic.

"If you win your division, you're in a good spot to win State," dad says.

"Yeah, I guess." This conversation could literally go on for the entire five hours if mom and dad choose to speculate about the outcome of State Cup. I'm not sure she does it on purpose, but she moves the conversation or inquisition away from State Cup and back to the game we just won.

"Sara, you showed a lot of composure on your breakaway. Great goal," my mom said.

"Thanks Mrs. Malone," Sara responds.

My mom continues with the compliments saying, "Janie your cross to Abbey was perfect."

"Thanks," says Janie.

My dad includes me in the kudos by adding, "Kate, you did a nice job switching the field today."

"Thanks dad."

Madi isn't left out. My parents are obsessed, but at least they spread the wealth of compliments. "Your throw-ins were amazing. Almost like corner kicks," adds mom.

"Thanks," Madi replies.

They seemingly gloss over the highlights and start a new angle of commentary of which we are not interested. Dad says, "So why didn't you form a wall for that direct kick?"

"What direct kick?"

"You know the one right before the half?"

I look at my teammates, no one really remembers it. "Nope,"I say.

"How do you not remember it? They almost scored! That's why I'm wondering why you didn't form a wall."

"I don't know Dad. Ask Coach Tom."

Then my mom pipes up, "Kate, do you think you could have gotten your head on that corner if you ran to the back post instead?" Geez! You'd think we lost the game. If my parents weren't going to stop on their own, we would have to force them. The IPod goes on and we zone out and stop answering them. How did the ride go so quickly on the way there?

Accompanying mom to the grocery store is a rare event for me. I hate running errands and mom says that I can't complain about the food we have at home if I don't come and help. For the most part, I don't. Today I was lured into the car not knowing a grocery run is on the "to do" list.

"Mom, can't you drop me back off at home before you go to the grocery store?" I ask.

"No. That doesn't make any sense. The grocery store is on our way home," mom replies.

"But I still have homework,"

"This won't take long. Especially with your help," she says with a smile.

The bakery greets us as we enter the store. There are so many delicious treats, I can hardly believe it. I pick up a tin of cinnamon rolls.

"How come we never have any of this stuff at home?" I ask.

"Because I don't like to have it in the house and you have never asked for it," mom explains.

"I didn't know they had all this stuff! I'm on sensory overload!"

"Well, pick out a few things and surprise your sister," mom says.

"Yes!" I place the cinnamon rolls in the cart. I grab some donut holes and pink icing cookies. Kelsey will be pleasantly surprised. I'm satisfied with my contribution.

"What do you want for dinner?" she asks.

"I don't care. No hamburgers though." We've had hamburgers like, three times this week.

"We are all actually home tonight for dinner. I have time to make something special if you want," mom offers.

"Ah, how about flank steak, mashed potatoes and Caesar salad?" I throw out the A-list menu.

"Yum! Sounds great. Let's find the fixin's," .

Meandering down the aisles, we see mom's friend, Debbie. "Debbie!" mom shouts and goes over to greet her friend. "Great to see you. How is the family?" mom asks.

"Super; I'm just running those boys around to baseball practice every day. Football is right around the corner. No break." In my mind, it's what every mom in our neighborhood says.

"No kidding," mom agrees.

Mrs. Murray greets me saying, "Hi Kate. How's soccer going?"

"Our season just finished."

"How did you do?"

"I don't know our record but we lost in the Semi's in State Cup," I explain.

"Oh, that's too bad."

"It's okay. We went up to Bellingham for the semi's and stayed in a hotel! My teammates and I ran around the hotel, painted our nails and swam. It was super fun."

"That *does* sound fun," she says to me. And, then she addresses my mom, "Sounds like she has her priorities straight," with a smile.

Mom teases back, "Yeah, a pretty expensive manicure." They laugh. I don't get it.

"Delicious meal Alyson; are we celebrating something?" dad asks as he starts to raise his glass.

"Just celebrating the fact we are all at the table together." Mom obviously misses these occasions.

"That's a good reason," dad says, "but hey, let's also raise our glasses to a great school year." He lifts his glass. We all do the same.

I chime in, "And a great soccer season!"

Kelsey says, "And to being one year closer to Jr. High!" We all laugh.

And mom caps it off, "To our family."

Part II

GRADE 9

CHAPTER TEN

Mom rouses me for the first day of school. "Rise and shine" she says with inflection in her voice. It's the same thing she has said since Kindergarten. Despite her annoying habits, this one does make for a nice way to start the day so I don't bite her head off about it. Actually, I'm surprised she had to come in at all. I am so excited for 9th grade I can't believe I didn't wake on my own. I've heard High School is *soooo* much better than Jr. High!

My new backpack is ready and I have a few outfits to choose from. I may have to text Morgan to find out what she decided to wear. I head over to my desk to grab my cell when I notice a new addition to the décor. It's a jelly jar filled with clovers! This has all the markings of a Joe Malone tradition in the works. There is a note next to the jar. In dad's distinctive handwriting smashed together to look like cursive, he explains why he left the batch of clovers:

"Hi Honey,
Sorry I missed you this morning. I had an early conference call. I'm leaving you this jar of clovers to help you mark the milestone of the first day of High School. My instruction for you is to invoke the power of the clover to set some goals and wishes for the upcoming year. Take some time this first week to consider what you want for yourself and how it might look.

Do your imagery and feel the feelings. Remember, you can write your own story. I can't think of a better way for you to start this new adventure! Have a great day at school. See you tonight.
Love, Dad"

Oh dad. So philosophical and thoughtful and basically giving me a homework assignment before I even start the first day of school! I'll think about it later, I need to figure out what to wear!

My freshman English teacher must have just been to some "teacher training" or something. She introduces the new school year with extraordinary enthusiasm. She is excited about teaching Julius Caesar, she has some fun brain exercises for us and most importantly, we all will become a "community of learners". So the first step toward building a community of learning is that we all must participate in creating the "classroom rules". A collective "eye roll" occurs and Ms. Miller asks for volunteers. Morgan raises her hand right away. She is a good rule follower. Her offering, "Respect each other".

Excellent choice I think to myself.

Our classmates add: "Be on time; no cheating; no gum; no bad hair," we all laugh at that one.

When the ideas peter out, Ms. Miller suggests the final and crucial rule: "Follow all school rules at ALL times!" Which, in teacher-speak means; NO cell phones, no electronics! By the looks of the classroom décor I can only assume that our newly hammered out rules will appear on the walls reminding us of our agreement with Ms. Miller. They will most certainly be laminated like all of the affirmations and teacher-isms that currently plaster the walls. It looks like a laminating machine barfed all over the place.

Ms. Miller isn't rationing her new ideas. After the classroom rules are voted in, she introduces her new brain stimulating exercise called, "divergent thinking". It is supposed to get our brain juices flowing. From now on we will do it on Wednesdays to kick start class. It goes like this: Ms. Miller gives us a term, phrase or symbol and we write down as many things that come to mind as we can. The goal is to come up with an answer no one else in the class offers. For example, she says, "rainbow". And we would write down the most creative answers we can think of; like, "colors", "arc", "treasure", and "gay pride". Then, we go around class and choose an original answer from our list without duplicating one that has been shared. Once your answer is shared, you are out. The person with the most original answer wins. The prize is an upgrade on an assignment. So, if we win, we can upgrade a paper from a C to a B or a B- to an A-. It is a huge prize so there is a lot of incentive to be creative.

Well, I sit next to a girl named Mandy. She has auburn hair that always looks a little tousled but pretty at the same time. Her eyes are kind yet wise, as if she's lived this life before. Mandy is so comfortable in her skin that it is almost intimidating. Not very many freshman girls have that kind of confidence. I remember her from Jr. High. We aren't friends. She hangs with a different crowd. I hear that her mom lets her throw parties when she is away on business. But, I've also heard that she gets good grades too. Boy, street smart, book smart and pretty; the trifecta. For posterity, I best come up with a more creative answer than Mandy since I go right before her.

Ms. Miller announces the divergent thinking question as merely: "28". My mind goes blank. I'm fairly creative, but the pressure of performing on the spot is too much. And, let's just say, I am still staying "close to the vest" with my creativity. I wrote: "Days in Feb (non leap year of course)" and I wasn't alone, nearly half the class was eliminated. David said, "Age of my uncle." I guess we can't prove it, but okay, that's original. Of course: "7 times 4" was a popular answer. And then it is Mandy's turn and she cleverly takes a breath, pauses and reveals her answer, "the number of pills in my birth control case". Game over. OMG. High School is way better! Wait till I tell my buddies about this!

I saunter in from school and mom is full throttle in the kitchen. "We're having family dinner on the first day of school?" I ask with some attitude.

"Yes, why not? No homework or practice. Dad and I want to hear all about it," mom says without responding to the attitude.

"What are we having?" I ask with a little more charm..

"Spaghetti," mom offers confidently.

"Spaghetti? We always have spaghetti," I say, but I'm likely pushing it with my mom.

"Well, we are having it again." Her tone indicates that I am on the verge of trouble.

Yet, I flirt with danger and ask, "Garlic bread?"

"Yep," she offers in a curt response.

"Good," I say heading toward my room.

Mom hollers after me asking, "How was your day?"

"Fine; you can hear about it at dinner."

Mom spruces up the usual meal with some freshly grated parmesan and homemade Caesar dressing. The spaghetti is delicious but I'm not going to say anything. But dad does, "As usual, great dinner. Thanks Alyson." Mom smiles as he acknowledges her effort.

"Girls, tell us about the first day of school. Kelsey, how was Jr. High?" mom asks.

"Awesome. It is so fun having a locker and different teachers, she says. Kelsey has been waiting in the wings for this day.

Mom continues her inquiry, "Do you like your teachers?"

"For the most part they seem cool. But the best part is lunch! I saw a whole bunch of girls from sports that I forgot would be at my school. We ate together with some of my friends from elementary school," Kelsey explains. It sounds more inclusive than *my* experience in 7th grade. Of course, she doesn't have the Devyn factor to contend with.

"Fantastic. I'm glad you are mingling," mom says with a sound of relief in her voice.

"What about you Kate? How is high school?" dad probes.

"Totally awesome," I say, "except, I don't have lunch with Morgan this semester, which sucks."

"Hey, watch your language," mom admonishes.

"Sorry. But, yeah, I have some good classes. My English teacher is really *enthuuusiastic*." I draw out "enthusiastic" for effect.

"What do you mean?" asks dad.

"Oh, she just went to some advanced teacher training and has all these ideas." I will not mention the divergent thinking exercise until I have a less controversial outcome.

"That's always good," mom suggests.

"I guess. We'll see."

"Any word on finding a high school soccer coach?" dad asks.

"It's the first day, Dad! And, it's a winter sport anyway."

"So true. Well, with that off the table, we'll just focus on your grades." He smiles offering a sarcastic spin on the comment.

"Yeah, yeah, yeah."

The interrogation dies down and we have a successful family dinner. I can't wait to retire to my room. "Thanks for dinner, mom". I get up to leave.

"Dishes, Kate",

I moan, "No first day of school reprieve?"

"Nope!" she says almost too happily.

"Knock knock." It's my dad at the bedroom door.

"I still don't know when soccer tryouts are," I joke.

"Funny. I actually am wondering if you read my note this morning," he asks.

"Oh yeah, the clovers. Yes, I remember my assignment," I respond.

"Have you thought about it?" dad asks.

"Again, first day! No homework on the first day, Dad." He's beginning to annoy me.

"It isn't intended to be a chore. I am hoping you will use it as a roadmap for your year." Then he adds, "But, it's up to you."

"I'll do it Dad. But maybe, I'll just make my wishes as I go along and not have a big plan." It's a compromise.

"Like I said, it's your choice. It was just an idea. Sleep well," he says closing the door behind him.

"Thanks, night Dad." I offer as my bedroom door clicks shut. I'm glad he didn't push it. However, I suppose I can come up with something. High school soccer tryouts are top of mind. I grab a clover and label it. My visualization is easy because I really feel confident already. It has been a goal of mine to make the high school team so that is a good start.

Chapter Eleven

Our final Premier practice for a few months ends. As we disband and grab our packs, Coach Tom hollers, "Stay healthy, no injuries!" I know these are not the only parting wishes he intends but his distress about having to "let us go" for a few months while we all go play soccer for our high schools is coming through. He's been training us since 7th grade and now he has to share us with another coach. Our skill set and health are in jeopardy! He promises to come watch us play and we believe him. In fact, it will be weird to play against my teammates. If all goes well Abbey and Claire will be at Interlake, Priya at Sammamish, Courtney and Sydney at Skyline, Hannah at UPrep, Cameron and Emily at Sacred Heart and Sara, Madi and I at Bellevue. I wonder if it will be an advantage to know their moves, or not?

Anyway, he's all nervous about it and we are all jazzed up about it. There doesn't seem to be the same sense of pressure or nerves for the tryout. I don't think its artificial confidence. We all should really make one of the teams: Frosh, JV or Varsity. Varsity! Wouldn't that rock? Really the only variable holding us back would be a bad attitude or acting like prima donnas. I'm not planning on exhibiting either. We all wave to Tom, almost shrugging him off. I think he's worrying for nothing.

Remarkably the sun is out but you wouldn't know it, it's like 30 degrees outside; but sunshine in January is a treat. Pretty good conditions for soccer and the much anticipated tryouts are providing the entertainment I expected; starting with the coach. Apparently she played in college, like 100 years ago! She looks about my mom's age and still fairly fit. She's definitely organized or so it seems by the clipboard she alternates holding on her hip or directly in front.

"Hello ladies. I'm Coach Kelly. You may call me Coach Kelly but not, 'Kelly,' okay? I teach math at the International School but there's no soccer team so I am excited to join BHS as the Girls' Varsity Soccer Coach. I will be supervising tryouts along with the JV coach, Coach Bradley." A small, athletic man in soccer sweats steps forward and waves. Coach Kelly continues, "We expect tryouts to last a few days and then we will post the results the old fashioned way… on the door to the girls locker room. Any questions?"

That was a mistake. Arms fly into the air. "How many girls are you taking?" girl *A* asks.

"Can't say; we'll put together the best squads," Coach Kelly answers.

"Do you want to know what position we play?" girl *B* asks.

"No, I will decide what position you play." Coach Kelly is succinct.

"What about goalie?" girl *C* asks.

"Let me know if you have any goalkeeping experience," is her response. Her answers are direct and confident. Coach Bradley nods along with her responses.

"Will the results list our real names on it or just our tryout numbers?" girl *B* asks.

Coach responds in her usual succinct manner, "Real names in alphabetical order."

Wow, hard core. And then, to dilute her alpha-coach jargon

Coach Kelly preempts our response by saying, "Unless you aren't comfortable with that."

It is such an assortment of players. Madi, Sara and I exude a level of confidence that is earned through years of practice, championship games and inclement conditions like rain, snow and the occasional heat wave. It doesn't take long for Coach Bradley to escort a group of girls to the other half of the field. Our group spends most of the tryouts scrimmaging.

I lean over to Madi as Coach Kelly gets us organized. "This is actually fun. I feel like Mia Hamm!" I say.

"No kidding. Not the competition we are used to, huh?" Madi says.

"Nope, but I like it. Less pressure, more fun!" I reply.

"I heard the Varsity team gets new uniforms this year. What number are you going to pick?" Madi asks.

"Don't jinx us, Madi!"

"Oh, we're fine. Look at Sara over there coaching those girls!"

I lean over and ask Madi, "What do you suppose Sara's saying?"

"Something like: 'Sorry to be presumptuous, but it would be my pleasure to explain how to defensively trap using the off-sides rule.' "

"Yeah, giving them tricks to defend against you and me!"

"That's Sara, trying to even the playing field for the betterment of mankind!"

"While improving their vocabulary in the process!"

Any lack of excitement during our high school soccer practice is compounded by Coach Kelly's style. It started with her very coordinated track suit and brand new cleats. Pulling yourself out of retirement, huh? And then, as if she had been scouting micro-soccer practices, she introduces our warm up which we will do daily. Per her enthusiastic instructions we must, "Follow the leader around the field: alternate side stepping, weaving through each other and high knees". It is so babyish we want to die! And by Wednesday, it was already Madi's turn.

"Madi, you lead!" Coach Kelly proclaims. Madi rolls her eyes at me horrified that someone might think she designed the warm up.

Before we start running the perimeter of the field I lean over to Madi and say, "Hopefully Coach Kelly doesn't join us again today. How embarrassing. Like, we can't run our own warm up!"

"I know," she whispers. "We've been playing soccer for like, 10 years. I think we know what to do!"

"Well, Leader," as I inflect some sarcasm, "Lead us!"

The sidelines present themselves before us and we jog out our warm up. As I run and mull over how I'm going to handle an entire season with Coach Kelly, our luck changes. Our babyish warm up is hardly fine-tuned; yet, with the precision of a military unit, the entire squad turns our heads toward the locker rooms at the same time. What appears in the short distance, in all their glory, is the boy's lacrosse team, heading toward the big field. The field that we are running around like 6 year olds! Not a player misses the pros and cons of the situation. Without a word, we pick up the pace to get all the way around the field before the boys reach it.

Coach Kelly looks up and yells out, "Oh yeah, we need to share the field with boys lacrosse for a while." A few moans. She better be kidding.

Sharing the field is the silver lining to the torturous practices Coach Kelly runs. If I'm not entirely humiliated by playing "Sharks and Minnows" arguably, a soccer drill designed for 1st grade rec players then I hope for some attention from the cute lacrosse players across the field. They seem pretty focused, unlike our side, which steals glances at every opportunity. Plus, there are lots of chances to zone out with Coach Kelly treating us like babies.

"Okay ladies," she says which is ironic, because she should be saying, "Okay babies." She continues on with some description about being "goal-side" on defense. I take a leap of faith and decide I don't have to listen. My eyes wander across the field.

It's hard to tell exactly who is who with their gear on, but everyone knows Ryan Lambert and Ty Fisher. I am willing one of them to look over so I can smile. But who's kidding who? It would take all of my courage to lock eyes with one of those gods. It doesn't matter anyway because they are actually listening to their coach.

Coach Kelly catches my attention wandering and shouts, "Kate, focus!"

"Oh, sorry Coach Kelly," I say respectfully. After all, she does control playing time.

CHAPTER TWELVE

I'm chillin' in my room waiting for Morgan to come over. We have an extra credit assignment to work on. I'm so glad we have some classes together because soccer is really keeping me busy. It's after dinner so when the doorbell rings my dad yells from his office, "Is someone expecting a guest or do I need to deal with a solicitor?"

I pop up and respond, "It's for me. It's Morgan. She and I are working on an extra credit assignment."

"It's a little late, don't you think?" dad replies.

As I walk past his office heading for the front door I respond, "I know, but we have to make a cake for our Ides of March party tomorrow so we really couldn't do it in advance."

"Ides of March? It rings a bell. Remind me," he says.

"Hold on Dad, I need to let Morgan in."

"Hi Morgan. Come in. Did you bring the candy to decorate the Julius Caesar cake?"

"Yep! Here it is," she says, "I asked my mom to take me to the Sweet Shop in the mall but she had too much work to do. I brought what I could find in our baking drawer. I have some licorice for the hair, Red Hots for his mouth and a marshmallow for the nose. I brought some random sprinkles and stuff too. I'll show you in the kitchen."

"Okay, but first I need to explain the Ides of March to my

dad. Come with me." We enter the office and dad says hello to Morgan.

"Hi Mr. Malone, I mean, Joe." She always forgets that he wants her to use his first name.

I proceed, "So Dad, we are reading Julius Caesar in English class. The Ides of March refers to March 15th and in Shakespeare's *Julius Caesar* it is the day Brutus whacks Caesar."

"Whacks?"

"Yeah, he stabs him in the heart. We are going to make a dead Julius Caesar cake. Stab wound and all," I explain.

"Nice! I'm sure it will be appetizing!" dad jokes.

Morgan chimes in, "Yeah, so tomorrow is March 15th; 'Beware the Ides of March' Mr. Malone!" She's quoting the soothsayers warning to Julius Caesar in the play.

My dad answers back, "Well, since I don't seem to have any political enemies at this time, I won't lose any sleep over the Ides of March!"

I see a stack of greeting cards and ask, "What are you doing, Dad?"

"I am writing out my St. Patrick's Day cards."

"You are sending out a lot." I say.

"Yeah, every year the list grows. Not everyone is 'officially' Irish that receives a card. I couldn't skip sending one to Mike."

I lean over to Morgan and whisper, "Mike is his tennis partner."

My dad turns on a big grin and says, "Look at how I addressed Mike's card."

I read the envelope, MR. MIKE MC HARRIS. I smile. Then I explain it to Morgan. "His name is Mike Harris. Dad added the "Mc" to be clever." Dad is quite happy with himself. I say, "Funny, Dad," but I'm really thinking, "Dorky!"

Morgan and I head to the kitchen and start making our Julius Caesar cake. I love hanging out with Morgan. She is a really agreeable girl, which makes being my friend easier as I can be a little demanding and I have some perfection issues. It's not that she is a pushover at all, she just is better at deciding what is important to fight for. I think of her as the Yin to my Yang- a complementary pair.

We are just short of starting a food fight in the kitchen. It is so much fun baking. Flour is everywhere. We had to start over once because we used one cup of salt instead of one tablespoon in the batter. Thank goodness we like to taste test or else we might have poisoned our class!

With the batter perfected, we put some white cake batter in a round cake pan and a rectangle cake pan. Just as we put the cake in the oven to bake, Kelsey joins us in the kitchen.

"Can I help?" she asks with eagerness.

"Just finished," I answer.

"Kate! Why didn't you tell me you were starting? Mom said I could help you."

"Mom doesn't know. This is our school assignment; you can't help."

"She said I could," Kelsey insists.

"You wanna help? You can do the dishes." I fan my arms out displaying the mess we made.

"You are so mean!" Kelsey declares.

"You are a little gnat," I reply. This is a new spin on calling her "annoying."

She tailspins and screams out, "Mom! Kate called me a brat."

"No, I didn't. I called you a gnat."

"Same thing," Kelsey contends.

"No it's not," I reply.

She marches off but doesn't return. I hope my mom talks her down and doesn't make me apologize in front of my friend.

In disbelief, Morgan says, "Wow. That's intense. My brother is so much younger than me. We don't fight like that."

"Yeah, we are only two years apart. It's not always like that though."

Sure enough, my mom calls me to the back of the house. "Kate was that really necessary?" she asks.

"Probably not," I admit.

"Can you please go in and say sorry?" She is asking, but really *telling* me to do it.

I turn to Morgan and explain, "My mom never takes 'no' for an answer." I had to get that out there so she understands why I must march in there and apologize.

In an effort to remind me my mom says, "Kelsey just likes to hang out with you, okay? She would walk on coals to be part of your fun." Mom always seems to take her side.

"Why doesn't she have her own friends?" I ask in frustration.

"She does. But every now and then, could you please include her without a fight? She's your sister."

Mom never had an annoying sister so she'll never understand. But, I have no leverage so I somberly say, "Okay."

I knock on the door and enter Kelsey's room. I immediately feel badly. She is playing her DS but I can't imagine she's winning the game because tears are streaming down her face. With as much sincerity as I can muster I say, "Kelsey, I'm sorry for calling you a gnat."

"That's okay," she says meekly. She is so forgiving! So, I feel like I should offer her something in return.

"The cake is almost done. You want to come help us with the decorating?"

Her face brightens as she exclaims, "Sure!" How easily she can turn the page.

"But remember, it's our project. We have to do most of the work."

"Got it," she agrees.

After a brief discussion we decide that we'll just cut out appendages from the rectangle cake. It's pretty funny trying to construct a "man" out of white cake. We are definitely not ready for *Ace of Cakes* quite yet! We laugh about our inadequacy! The Julius Caesar looks like a snowman, but we are hoping the hair and eyes and of course the knife piercing his heart will make the concept more believable. The frosting helps bring it all together as the individual pieces are disguised by the layer of yummy cream cheese frosting which is painted on as a toga. We each try to make a flesh color for the face and legs. Kelsey's batch comes out the least yellow-ish so we use it. Using candy for the facial features makes it look even more absurd and even more like a snowman. We are giggling our way through this project! Luckily there isn't a rubric attached to this extra credit assignment. We assume that just showing up with it is enough. The doorbell rings and Morgan's mom is here to take her home. Bummer! So, the finishing touch is the plastic knife piercing the white, fluffy heart. I assure her the cake will make it to class in one piece.

"Kate, see you tomorrow! Bye Kelsey!" Morgan looks back and reminds us, "Beware the Ides of March!"

Cursed by the Ides of March, I am scrambling to get ready for school. I slept right through my alarm. I knew I should have geared up a louder song on my IPod! It is a game day and I have to get my soccer gear together too. Dang!

"Mom! I need a ride to school today!" I yell from my room, a legitimate distance from the kitchen.

"What?" she asks.

"I need a ride!"

I hear her walking down the hall toward my room. "You know I hate it when you holler at me from back here. I can't hear you with the dishwasher and TV on. What do you need?"

"A ride," I say again.

"Why?" mom asks. Doesn't she know what time it is?

"I'm running late and I have my soccer pack and my back pack. And, oh crap, the Ides of March cake too!"

"Language! Fine, fine; I will throw some clothes on." As she is scurrying away, she says, "You are lucky I don't have any appointments this morning!" What, an appointment with laundry? Whatever, just get me to school on time, I have a cake to deliver!

"Remember, drop-off is at the back of the school," I say.

"Yep, I remember."

"Thanks Mom."

"Sure."

I open the car door and start loading up my bags on my body in any way that will free up my arms to carry the cake. I surely do not want my mom to help me bring anything in. I am groveling with my pack mule system and can't get the car door shut. I lift my leg to slam it shut with my foot when an arm reaches around and shuts it for me.

"Need some help?" a male voice asks. Clearly I do. But, when I look up to see that it is Ryan Lambert, lacrosse god, I stammer.

"Ah, sure, thanks."

"Whatcha got going on here?" Ryan asks.

"It's a cake for our party in Language Arts."

"You want me to carry it?" he offers.

"Ah, sure. Thanks." "Where we headed?" he inquires.

"The 400 wing."

"No prob. So, how is soccer going?"

"It's been a bumpy season. We haven't won a game yet," I hesitate to admit. "How did you know I play soccer?" I ask, wondering if he will say, 'Because I've noticed you at soccer practice?'

Ryan replies, "Cuz you're wearing your soccer sweatshirt and carrying your soccer stuff?"

OMG! I'm such an idiot! "Oh, yeah," I smile. Of course he didn't notice me. "We play Mercer Island tonight," I add.

"Cool. Good luck," he says.

Ryan's encouragement has more impact than a fistful of clovers! "Thanks."

I nudge open the classroom door and gesture Ryan towards an empty table. He lifts the foil and looks quizzically at our creation.

"What the heck?" Ryan says.

"Oh, don't even go there. I'll explain it some other time," I say as I try to blow it off.

"Looks like it might taste good anyway!" he says with a cute smile on his face.

And, off he goes. My 15 minutes of fame with Ryan Lambert.

"Were you guys playing soccer or rugby tonight?" dad asks after the game.

"I know. I'm beat up. The refs weren't calling anything!" I say bitterly.

"Better to be beat up with a win, than beat up with a loss!" dad says.

"No kidding," I agree.

"That one goes into 'ugly win' category. But, a 'W' is a 'W'. Your first win this season! Good job!" Dad definitely likes his "W's"!

"That was a sweet goal from Sara, huh?" I ask.

"Absolutely. But, that was a sweet pass you dished right to her. Don't forget about that!" Dad is always propping me up.

"I didn't! Dad, you know how Sara has such a funny way of talking sometimes?"

"Like an adult, you mean?"

"Yeah. Wanna hear what she said after the game? She's so funny."

"Shoot," Dad says.

"So, we are all psyched about the win and reviewing all the great plays and dissing M.I. and she interrupts us to say, 'Friends and teammates. This victory tonight propel us into a winning streak!' Propel us—isn't she funny?"

Dad laughs, "She is always good for a quick grammar or vocabulary lesson, huh?"

"Yep. I like her."

"Me too," dad says. "And, she might be onto something. A winning streak sounds good!"

I reply, "Fat chance with our lame coach."

"Kate!" dad exclaims.

"Sorry Dad but it's true. You should see how she runs practices. It reminds me of practices when I was a Tiger!"

"That orange jersey team when you were six or seven?" he says with a chuckle at my exaggeration.

"Yes!"

"Coach Kelly is doing her best," dad replies. I think he sincerely believes so.

"But we are just limping along with ineffective practices and no intensity during the games," I divulge.

"How can you help change that?" dad inquires.

"I don't know."

"You are a team leader, Kate. I'm sure there is something you can do. She's basically volunteering her time. You might want to start by being more forgiving of her."

"I thought you were more competitive than that?" I ask with a puzzled look on my face.

"Oh, don't get me wrong. I love to watch you win," he quickly replies.

"Dad, I just assumed we would have the same kind of success as my Premier team."

"That can still happen if you give up the willingness to believe she is a poor coach," dad proclaims.

"It's not just that I believe she is a poor coach; she actually is!"

"If you can say with certainty that it is absolutely true that Coach Kelly is a poor coach, then go ahead and stick with that belief. But, I suggest you change your thinking around first and see what happens." I'm starting to think this advice is leading back to dad's manifestation concept. Like many of my dad's philosophical "nuggets" this too will require some pondering. "Okay. I'll start there. I'm going to clean up and go to bed. I'm tired. Good night, Dad."

I lay in bed considering dad's advice. I suppose it isn't all her fault that we aren't winning. Just because the practices aren't super stimulating, doesn't mean I couldn't try focusing more. In fact, the whole team could focus more. I'll be a better leader in that regard. Plus, we did win tonight. Coach Kelly moved some players out of their normal positions which had favorable results. It was a good move to put Sara at forward tonight since no one else could get through the defender; that resulted in her making our winning goal. Coach Kelly also gives me a ton of playing time which I agree with. I laugh to myself. I guess I was a little unfair to call her "lame" after all.

I'm looking for Coach Kelly before practice starts. She isn't in the locker room so I venture up the stairs into the Athletic office. Crouched in front of the smallest and most outdated TV I've ever seen is Coach Kelly. The images on the screen are soccer players, but not us. The jerseys are green and white, not blue and gold.

I know I'm interrupting but I need to talk to her so I blurt out, "Hi, Coach."

"Hi Kate. Great game last night!"

"Thanks. It was so fun to win."

"I agree! I knew you girls could do it. It's just been harder for me to help you girls gel than I had thought it would be," Coach says.

"Oh, you are doing a great job though, Coach." I actually believe it as I'm saying it.

"Well, I'm trying. I actually snagged this DVD of the Issaquah girls, who we play next week. They have some really good players, but I will find some holes."

"Wow. That's a lot of work. Thanks." I *am* grateful.

"No problem. I love it, and I want to win just as much as you guys," she admits.

"Cool. Hey, I was thinking that it might be fun for us players to run a practice every now and then," I suggest. "Maybe pair us up and we have to put together a plan and execute it on Fridays or the day after a game?"

"That's an interesting idea. Have you talked to any of the players about it?" Coach asks.

"No, not yet; I just thought of it last night before I fell asleep."

"I like it, but you would have to show me the plan in writing. It's harder than you think to fill up an hour and a half," Coach warns.

"That's fine." A plan in writing shouldn't be a big deal I think to myself.

"Also, you would have to have practice goals," Coach says. "Work your plan around something you think the team needs to work on like, corner kicks or give and go's, for example."

Maybe running a practice requires more planning than I thought. "I'm not sure the gals will want to go to that much work. Never mind!" I say.

"Wait a sec. What if you modify your idea and still pair up but only run the last half hour of practice or create a new warm up? That would help me a lot," Coach says. "I'd love to get some ideas, especially from you girls that play off season for other coaches."

"That sounds better; and manageable," I respond. "The girls would have strangled me for signing them up for all that work! You wanna bring it up or should I?"

"I'll carve out some time at the end of practice and you can share it with the team. Sound good?"

"Sounds great; thanks Coach Kelly!" I'll do my part to make a winning streak a reality. With this better mindset, I already feel like I've won.

CHAPTER THIRTEEN

It's time for me to have a boyfriend. On the general teenage "timeline", I'm years behind but I just haven't been ready. As I lay in bed trying to fall asleep, I can't quite put a finger on my trepidation. I have enjoyed crushes on boys but I've never quite mustered the ability to actually impress a boy enough to ask me out. It's true that I put up this façade of "being too busy" to bother with boys. After all, my flourishing soccer career takes a lot of time, right? Oh please; I would love a boyfriend but, truth be told, I'm nervous. I like the attention from boys but I'm not sure what to do with a one on one relationship! Some girls, like Devyn, just ooze femininity and the confidence to attract a boyfriend. Is there a clinic for such a skill set?

As I start to fall asleep I decide to put the clover tree to a big test. A boyfriend! There you go! I press the clover labeled "Kate's boyfriend" to the tree. I lay back and think about what it will look like for me; Kate Malone, to have a boyfriend. While it may not look like everyone else's version—it will be mine. Safe, honest, trustworthy and all the butterflies to go with it!

Devyn is my Brutus. Today, St. Patrick's Day is normally one of my favorite holidays. Dad's enthusiasm is contagious and we can count on his early morning greeting, "The Irish are at their best when there is something to celebrate; Happy St. Patrick's Day girls!" On a typical day, he's long gone to work by the time Kelsey and I get going in the morning, but on St. Patrick's Day he lingers to make green scrambled eggs with bacon and show off his newest shamrock tie. The internet has been a blessing for dad and his annual quest for a new tie. This year's is particularly obnoxious because an Irish jingle resonates from the bottom of the tie when you press it. Fortunately dad doesn't break into a jig but as always, it is a festive morning and presumably a festive day. That is, until Devyn's antics ruin it.

It isn't hard to notice them; a flock of girls, many of them my friends. They are cruising campus in matching St. Patrick's Day outfits. At the front of the pack is Devyn, prancing like a Queen Bee in green sweats from Pink, shamrock bandana around her head and green beads around her neck.

"C'mon girls," Devyn announces, "let's walk through the locker bay one more time!"

I see Morgan trailing the group a bit. She has the beads and bandana but no matching sweats like everyone else. I feel sick. I run for cover. I dare not let them see me. I wanna cry. I scoot behind a pillar. Morgan sees me, comes over looking sheepish and says, "Hey Kate."

Even though she's one of my best buddies, I'm blunt and say, "Nice outfit," with a sarcastic inflection in my voice.

"Yeah, well, Devyn just handed me these things and told me to put them on. It's weird," Morgan replies.

"Do you know what's going on?" I ask, continuing my directness.

"Kinda."

"What?" She better tell me before I lose it.

"I guess Devyn hosted a sleepover last night and they all got those outfits to wear today," Morgan explained.

"On a school night?" I ask, puzzled by the idea.

"Yeah, I know. It's weird," Morgan says, "my mom would never let me go."

"I know, mine either. And Devyn would have just made fun of me for not being able to attend," I said with a solid knowingness.

"Yeah me too; I think I just got this stuff cause I got off the bus when they were arriving this morning and Devyn saw me," said Morgan.

"Well, at least you weren't totally left out. I feel kind of stupid," I admit.

"Maybe she plans to give you something at lunch?" Morgan offers.

"Maybe, we'll see." It's Devyn though, so I'm skeptical. I've been looking over my shoulder because of her since 7th grade. She is Brutus: shifty, manipulative and a traitor.

I sit next to Morgan at the lunch table. No one acts like there is anything wrong. Hello! I'm over here, dressed normal! There is no offering at lunch; "Et tu, Devyn?"

Mom is the first set of ears to listen to my story of woe. "It was so humiliating. They were all dressed alike, and then there's me; at the end of the table, feeling stupid. And, in every period, there was at least one person from the posse to remind me that I was left out!" My mom can't get a word in, "And, guess what?"

"What?" mom asks, not really having any other choice.

"They conspired to wear the outfits at a sleepover last night!"

"Really? Where?"

"At Devyn's house, of course," I say with disgust.

"That makes sense. Even so, I find it hard to believe that Carly's mom would let her go to a sleepover on a school night," mom replies.

"I know. The whole thing is weird, Mom, right?"

"Well, maybe it was planned last-minute."

"Doubtful. It looked pretty organized to me."

"What about Morgan?" mom asked.

"Morgan bumped into the crew before school and they gave her some stuff."

"What about Madi?"

"Madi wasn't at school today. Her mom took her to the doctor to check out her knee injury from the game."

Mom reminds me, in an effort to make me feel better, by saying, "You know I wouldn't have let you go anyway, right?"

"Yeah, I know."

"But, it just would have been nice to be invited, huh?" mom asks with a sound of sincere sympathy in her voice.

My eyes well up as I squeak out, "Yeah."

Mom hugs me and promises, "Tomorrow will be a better day. I know it."

It may be High School and no longer Jr. High but the lunchroom dynamic is the same. Most of the learning happens during the lunch hour amidst the eating, gossiping, flirting and observing. As I approach the lunch table dozens of eyes looked in my direction. Devyn is scowling at me. By now, I'm accustomed to her bizarre reactions. She hates when someone else has the spotlight. But, somehow her energy feels different today.

The table is all abuzz. Apparently, Ryan Lambert asked Madi for my phone number in between classes. OMG! She told him she would have to ask me first even though she knew I had an enormous crush on him. Geez, get him that number ASAP! So, lunch hour proceeds with me and my friends considering every possible scenario of my first contact with "Hot Ryan". I am hoping the actual contact will be as exciting as the anticipation of it!

The expected text came in on the bus ride home. "HEY

KATE, THAT'S TIGHT THAT UR SOCCER TEAM CRUSED M.I."

I want to text back right away but I have to show Sara and Madi first, who are on my bus.

"Sara, OMG, Ryan just texted me about our soccer team!"

"Let me see," she says.

"Omigosh!" she exclaims. Ryan just texted YOU!"

"I know, I know," I say. Thank goodness I had some warning that the text was coming because I am totally overwhelmed as it is.

"You guys, I just need to text back, okay?" The urgency is overwhelming.

"What are you going to say?" asks Sara.

"I don't know…" as I look at my text screen and formulate an answer.

So I quickly reply back, "YA, COOL WIN. NOT MANY WINS THIS YEAR THO. WERE U THERE?" Very safe, I thought.

He sends back, "YA. U ROCKED. U WANNA HANG OUT SOMETIME?"

"Holy crappers," I say loudly. "Ryan just asked me out…I think!"

Madi grabs my phone. Sara is hovering over her. "OMG!" they scream in unison.

I'm the first between us to foray into the boyfriend thing; I think they are happy and nervous for me!

Madi reminds me, "Text back, text back!"

"Oh, okay. Can one of you please call Morgan? Tell her what's going on!" I ask out of necessity.

Instead, Sara quickly sends a text to Morgan. They are going back and forth.

Meanwhile, I send the following reply to Ryan, "THAT'D BE COOL." Off it goes!

In an instant I get the following reply, "COOL. MEET @ THE CLUB TO SHOOT HOOPS FRI NITE?"

Oh wow, a real date Friday night! My friends are frenzied too!

They mimic my own conclusion. "Kate, *ohhhh*, Friday night!" says Madi.

Sara starts analyzing the logistics, "Have you considered how you will get there? Are you going to tell your mom and dad?"

"Hold on!" I say to stop the inquisition. I mentally scan my schedule. I think I'm free. My mom better not have me committed to anything that night. That's my last thought before I commit to Ryan by replying, "SOUNDS COOL. WHAT TIME?"

Sara reiterates her question, "Kate, are you going to inform your parents?"

"I don't think so. You guys are my cover and reinforcements. I need to tell Morgan to come too. Don't make any plans for Friday. I need you guys," I plea.

"Why aren't you going to tell your parents?" Sara asks.

"I don't know. I just don't want to make a big deal about it in case it doesn't work out."

"What do you mean?" Sara probes.

"Well, what if he doesn't show up or we don't have fun?" I assert.

"Still, Kate. They should know," Sara insists.

"Sara, it's just hoops at the club. Something I would do with you and Madi anyway. Just help me out on this. I'm a nervous wreck. I don't need my mom asking a million questions or my dad insisting on meeting Ryan first. I promise I will tell them if Friday goes well. Okay?"

"Okay. I'll be there," she agrees.

"Me too!" says Madi. "I wouldn't miss it!"

I send a text to Morgan about Friday night. She replies, "CALL ME WHEN U GET HOME . I'M OUT ON FRI. HAVE 2 BABYSIT. DANG!"

My cell vibrates and the final detail from Ryan waits: "7. CYA." My first date!

I'm heading toward 1st period LA and I see Ryan near the 300 wing. He executes a head nod in my direction. Is the nod for me? Do I dare look around to check? Oh crap. I decide on a smile and a half wave back. He smiles. It was for me. I float into class. I cannot remember finding my seat or anything my LA teacher said in class today. Lunchtime sneaks up and it's time to conspire with Madi and Sara about Friday night.

We are huddled together at the end of the lunch table working out the details and our secrecy hits Devyn's radar screen. "What's the big secret?" Devyn asks as she walks by.

"No secret," I lie. "We are just talking about the weekend."

"What's going on?" Devyn probes.

Madi and Sara look at me to answer since it is my news. "Oh, I'm hanging out with Ryan Friday night."

"Ryan Lambert?"

"Yep." I'm all smiles. I can't help it.

"Well, aren't you special?" she answers snidely.

I basically ignore her, like I usually do when she cops an attitude. Under my breath I say to Madi and Sara, "What is her problem with me?"

"You don't hover and grovel over the boys but you somehow managed to score a date with Ryan!" offers Sara.

"Does she like Ryan?" I ask.

"Everyone likes Ryan! Don't you get how awesome this is?" Madi adds.

"Yeah, I guess I do." Be careful what you wish for, huh? Clover tree, you came through for me ten-fold. Did you really have to choose the most popular boy in school for me? I'm under a microscope for my first date ever.

All my ducks are in a row. Mom is dropping me and my

reinforcements off at the club at 6:45PM. We hit a snag when my sister wants to join us. I'm in the middle of texting Madi to help me with my outfit, since I'm in angst over what to wear, when Kelsey comes bouncing into my room.

"What are you doing tonight?" Kelsey pries.

"Uh, I'm going to the club with Madi and Sara."

"Can I come?"

"No, I kinda want to chill with my friends alone."

"But, *Kaaate*, I can't find anyone to hang out with me. I don't have anything to do," Kelsey says in her most whiney voice ever.

"Not tonight," I sternly reply.

She starts to beg, "*Pleeease*. I'm in Jr. High now. I'm not a baby."

"Kelse, I don't have time for this."

"*Pleeease*."

"No, absolutely not."

Next, her anger kicks in as she proclaims, "You never want to hang out with me!"

I'm trying to stay calm, "Yes, I do. But we've had these plans all week."

"You are so mean! I'm going to ask mom if I can just go by myself then!"

Oh geez, I can't have that scenario. If mom agrees, then I'll surely get stuck with her at some point or worse yet, mom will walk her in and see what's up. OMG!

I don't want my parents involved so I have to tell Kelsey what is going on. I don't want to tell her who, but she is forcing my hand. Kelsey's reaction is a resounding, "No way! Ryan Lambert?" I don't know how she knows who he is but, whatever. "You have liked him forever!" and she is right.

"How do you know?" I ask.

"I don't know. I just have heard his name for a long time. You and your friends always talkabout him."

I'm imagining her with her ear sucked up to my closed bedroom door. I don't even want to know what else she's heard. I make a mental note to be more careful. But at this moment I need her to keep my secret. "You can't tell mom and dad but I'm meeting Ryan at the club tonight. Okay?"

"Okay. I don't know what the big deal is. I don't think they'd care."

"Who knows; that's just my plan and I'm sticking to it. Kelse, I've got to figure out my outfit; out!" Reluctantly, she leaves.

I ponder my options. Lululemon pants? The athletic club is one of the only places my parents let me wear them. My dad hates how form fitting they are but how can they ban exercise pants from an athletic club? My only other options are jeans or basketball shorts. Jeans, not good for exercise; hoop shorts, not cute; Lululemon it is. Finishing touches: hair in a pony, light mascara and my Northface vest. It's 6:30PM. On the outside, I'm ready. On the inside, I'm in shambles!

"Mom, it's time to go!" I holler from my room.

"Alright—meet you in the car," she hollers back.

Scurrying out of the house, my stomach in knots, I do not notice that the house is empty. As I hop in the car I notice Kelsey in the back seat.

"What are *you* doing in the car?" with emphasis on…"you".

"Hey, watch the tone," mom interjects.

"But I told her I was hangin' out with my friends…."

Kelsey interrupts, "Mom and I are going out for frozen yogurt."

"At the club?" I ask with a little too much concern.

"*Noooo,*" says Kelsey with some slight attitude. "I told mom that I'd rather try that new frozen yogurt place in the mall, Yogurtland!" She emphasizes it like it's a theme park. I'd think she was funny if I wasn't so stressed.

"Oh, okay," I respond. I'm so relieved. I might owe her. I text Madi and Sara: "WE R ALMOST THERE. B READY.. IT'S ALMOST 7!"

My mom says in a surprised tone, "Those girls look like sentinels waiting on the curb for us. I can't recall Madi ever being ready and waiting!"

"Yeah, Sara's just a good influence in general." I play it off, hoping I'm believable. I glance back and Kelsey is staring out the window with a "Cheshire" grin as mom pulls up to the curb.

"Hi ladies," mom says, greeting my friends first.

"Hi, Mrs. Malone!" they both respond as they clamor into the car.

I'm sending out into the universe all my "drive really fast and get good traffic signals vibes" during our ride towards my first date! It works pretty well but we are still cutting it close. Mom pulls into the parking lot and my stomach lurches. Holy crap! Ryan is walking right past our car! In a split second I think, "Please don't notice me; please don't notice me." But, he does. And, he waves.

The communication does not go unnoticed. "Who is that cute boy?" my mom inquires.

I am stressed and annoyed. "Ah, that's Ryan Lambert." I glance back and see the three of them stuck to the back seat; eyes bugged, motionless and freaking out for me.

"Does he go to your school?" Mom continues the inquiry.

"Yeah." Can we be done here? Please?

She responds, "Hmmm, Lambert. That sounds familiar. I don't know why." She is going to ramble on.

I cut her off and say, "He plays a lot of sports. That's probably it. Thanks for the ride Mom!"

"No problem sweetie. Dad or I will pick you up at 10:30. Have fun!"

Madi and Sara chime in with their gratitude, "Thanks Mrs. Malone!"

The car door barely closes when Madi and Sara flank me from each side. "Wow that was a close one!" Sara determines.

"Ryan looks *soooo* cute tonight!" says Madi

"You are *soooo* lucky Ryan didn't wait for you outside," Sara says.

"I bet he's waiting right inside the lobby!" Madi says with excitement in her voice.

"Okay, so we'll meet you back in the lobby at 10. K?"

"Yes, Sara, I'll be there."

"Good luck!" she says

"Good luck?" I ask

"I mean, have fun! Love you lots!"

"Remember everything!" Madi adds as I walk away and wave.

My wingmen peel off as we enter the club. Ryan is waiting for me and with a grin says, "Hey Kate."

"Hi Ryan," I respond as I fuss with my ponytail.

"Good drop off?" he asks with a snicker in his voice.

"What do you mean?" I ask while my nervous energy sends my hands once again to my ponytail. I release the hairband but reconnect my locks within seconds.

"You didn't tell your mom about me, huh?" he nudges me affectionately.

"No, I didn't tell my parents about tonight." I say with a renewed confidence because Ryan is so darn sweet.

"Thought so; why?"

"Well, they would insist on meeting you first and I didn't want to waste their time in case I didn't have fun tonight." I'm kidding of course, but I cannot believe that came out of my mouth!

"Good one," Ryan concedes with another fabulous smile. Ice is broken! "Wanna go shoot hoops?" Ryan offers.

"Sure!" I reply with my own fabulous smile.

Are you kidding that Ryan Lambert is teaching me how to shoot hoops? Every time his hand brushes mine I want to collapse. I've never properly shot a basketball in my life. There seems to be a lot of technique involved. "Kate, hold the ball like this, one hand bracing the ball and the other to guide."

"Okay." I do what he says.

"Bend your knees." I do that. "Okay, good. But stay straight." I follow his every direction.

"Now shoot." I bend my legs, hold my arms steady and fling the ball. It hammers off the backboard. Not even close. Okay, this is going to be a problem. I am an athlete. The cutesy, nervous girl that has taken over my body needs to depart! "What am I doing wrong? Okay, really, teach me how to shoot a basket," I implore.

Ryan is still laughing at my first try. And then, he realizes I am serious. "It was your first try! A little impatient, huh?"

"Not impatient, just competitive."

"Excellent! I like good competition."

"Is my form right?"

"Yep, you are fine. It just takes practice," he assures me.

"Let's see if I can get it in the hoop so we can play HORSE," I suggest.

"Game on. But let's see if I can be a good coach first," Ryan suggests.

This is the best first date! My shot hasn't improved dramatically, but I am catching on slowly. Ryan, patient as ever, is growing weary.

"Hey coach; can I buy you a smoothie?" I ask while I try out my underdeveloped flirtatious smile. It works.

He grins, grabs my shoulders and replies, "Sounds great!"

Ryan admits, "I wanted to buy *you* a smoothie tonight."

"You can buy next time. Thanks for being so patient, you know, teaching me how to shoot a basketball."

"No prob. I can't think of any other girl that would actually spend an entire evening learning to shoot hoops. That was cool. Next time we'll play HORSE, K?"

Next time! Yippee! "HORSE it is. I'd better schedule in some shooting practice in the mean time!"

"You'll pick it up fast. So, are you willing to introduce me to your parents now?" he asks.

"I suppose you passed the test. I'll introduce you to Joe and Alyson." I smile and check my phone. I have like, 50 texts from Morgan who is stuck babysitting and wants to know how it's going. I'll get back to her soon. But the time on my phone reads 10:15PM. Time flies when you are with a cute boy. "Oh, I gotta go hook up with Madi and Sara for our ride home."

Ryan boldly asks, "So, were they here to help you fool your parents or save you in case you wanted a bail out?"

"Both!" And, we both start laughing.

The prospect of being totally alone with a boy has me a little nervous. After school on Monday, I am going home with Ryan. He watches his little sister on Mondays while his mom works. I hope I don't say something stupid or find myself in an awkward position. I like Ryan a lot and I definitely get those jittery butterfly feelings when we are together but, I've never kissed a boy, and feel like I probably should have by now, and what if I do it wrong!

I text my mom after school so it seems more like a last minute plan. I tell her I'm staying for tutorial and will take the late bus home. She doesn't really ask very many questions, so it's an easy ploy. I feel badly that I'm not telling her the truth and I seem to be making a habit out of omitting information. But, I really wanted to tell Ryan "Yes" and I know for sure my mom wouldn't have let me go. So, with my lie in place, I meet Ryan at the lockers after school.

"I told my sister about you. She's excited to meet you," Ryan says.

"What's her name?" I ask.

"Ashley. Just to warn you, we will be adequately chaperoned by my six-year old sister!"

We tackle homework for a while, talk about soccer and then watch some TV side by side. Our shoulders touch and I seriously get the "wooziest" stomach. I cannot remember the show we are watching because all I think about is whether he will put his arm around me or lean over to kiss me. Inevitably his little sister bounds into the room, breaking up our close proximity. She is a cute kid and she immediately tags me as someone who might make crafts and play "restaurant" with her.

"Kate-y, can we make some cookies?" Ashley asks with a persuasively cute smile on her face.

I shoot Ryan a quick glance. As much as I like baking cookies, I much prefer the shoulder snuggle I was having with her brother. He gives it a weak effort, "Ashley, why don't you come in here and color instead?"

"Aw, Ry, please, please, please. I bet Katey makes the best snickerdoodles!"

It is his turn to glance over at me. I sigh and move to get up. Ryan squeezes my leg in gratitude and an electrical current of affection shoots throughout my body ending right in my heart!

"I'm in!" I say, somewhat enthusiastically. "Snickerdoodles are the perfect antidote to the rain outside. But, your brother may have to help bake them; I have to get home soon."

"Yea! Thanks Katey! You are the best!" Ashley exclaims.

I'm hoping that Ryan thinks so too!

Ashley and I roll out the last snickerdoodle and I notice the time. "Yikes, I need to go!" Ryan walks me to the door, "I'm sorry I can't walk you home, but I have to stay here with Ashley."

"That's okay," I say even though I don't mean it. Meandering home with Ryan would be great.

He leans toward me and I think I might faint. His arms encircle me and I can feel his muscular chest against mine. He whispers, "Ashley isn't the only one who thinks you are great."

I can barely breathe. "Thanks" and I pull away. Why did I

pull away? What an idiot I am! "Bye Ryan; text me later. And, bring me a snickerdoodle for lunch tomorrow!"

I could have been virtually transported back home because I don't even remember the walk. This is the best feeling in the whole world! My mom snaps me out of my delirium.

"Hi sweetie, how was tutorial?"

I don't think she suspects anything so I casually say, "Fine."

"That's good. I'm glad you don't have practice on Mondays anymore so you can take advantage of tutorial."

"Me too!" And I mean it!

I go into my room and flop on my bed. Ryan and I exchange texts for about an hour while my mom thinks I am doing more homework.

Apparently my mom has a larger network for information gathering than I anticipated. I am in my room after school finishing homework when she knocks on the door.

"Kate, do you have a sec?" The tone is different enough that I sense something is up. With my clandestine behavior lately, I should possibly brace myself. "Sure, come in."

"I bumped into Devyn's mom at the grocery store today." Gulp. That name is never associated with good news. "Yeah?" I say but cringe at the thought of the rest of the news.

"Apparently Devyn has a crush on that boy Ryan Lambert. You know—the one we saw at the club?"

"I heard that." This had all the markings of a set up. Starting with Devyn and ending with my mom.

"Well, she is quite upset that you have been hanging out with him."

I'm speechless yet my mind is racing wondering to what extent I'm busted.

"You know I don't like to be blindsided, Kate. Start from the beginning. And, I'm putting the pieces together that it wasn't a coincidence we saw him in the parking lot of the club."

"No, it wasn't. I did meet him there. We just shot hoops and had a smoothie. Madi and Sara were there if I needed a bail out."

"Good plan but why couldn't you tell dad and me?"

"Oh Mom, I was so nervous about it and I didn't want a big production before I spent some time getting to know him."

"From what I understand, he sounds like a nice kid. But, dad and I will expect you to introduce us to him before you see him again. Okay?"

"Okay," I reply. If I want to see Ryan again, it's inevitable.

"I'm not going to tell your dad about this. He's been talking about hazing your first boyfriend since the day you were born. He'll be upset if he knows you went on a date without his approval."

"It wasn't really a date, Mom."

"According to us, it qualifies" mom explains.

"Got it," I say.

"One freebie, Kate, but, don't lose our trust. Understand?"

"Yep. Thanks Mom." I know I should come clean about spending the afternoon alone with Ryan because she's being so cool but I can't muster the courage. In a split second decision I decide to roll the dice and hope she doesn't find out about it. The guilt I feel may be punishment enough. I better get Ryan over to charm my parents before I screw this whole thing up.

CHAPTER FOURTEEN

The new routine involves me flying off the bus in the morning to meet Ryan at my locker. He walks to school and can time it perfectly to our bus schedule. It's really the only time during the school day that we see each other. Hopefully next semester we will have lunch together, at least. I turn the corner it feels like a thousand eyes are on us. Having the entire school document our courtship is overwhelming.

"Good morning," I say.

"Hey there; I had fun yesterday," Ryan says with a playful nudge and yet another adorable grin.

"Me too, but I need you to meet my parents."

"That sounds official," Ryan states.

I stammer. "Ah, well, yeah, I guess."

"I'm just kidding, when?"

"It has to be before we hang out again according to my mom."

"Hey, I was thinking we should get a group together to go to the movies this weekend," Ryan offers.

"That sounds great! Who do you have in mind?" I ask.

"Why don't you get some girls together and I'll bring a group of guys. We can all hang out." Two thoughts; one, my friends are going to freak at their good fortune because Ryan's buddies are really cool too. And two, it's time to be unnerved about introducing Ryan to my parents.

"Pick me up for the movies and meet them right before?" I ask.

"I'll see if I can get the car."

"Cool." Regardless, I do not want my dad to drive us to the mall. I'd rather walk! The downside to being the older sister is that there is no road map for this sort of thing. I have no idea what the introduction will entail. My dad can be kind of dorky. Mom can be dorky too, but I expect she won't say much. This is dad's moment. Two daughters and no sons; this is his rite of passage too.

The door slams behind me, "Mom, I'm home!"

"In the office!" I head in that direction.

"Mom, am I available tomorrow night?"

"I can't hear you. Please come in here to talk."

"I'm coming." I stop in the doorway and mom looks up. "Am I free this weekend to go to the movies?"

"With Ryan?" she immediately inquires.

"Yeah, but a whole group of kids too."

"Like who?"

"Not sure yet. But he's gonna get some buddies and I'll bring Madi, Morgan and Sara; maybe Janie. Whoever can come, I guess."

"You know what needs to happen, right?" she asks.

"Yeah, I already told him he needs to meet you guys."

"Good. Saturday night would work. Dad and I are around."

"Cool, but Mom?"

"Yeah?"

"Can you please talk to Dad? Please do not let him embarrass me."

"He won't. He was a teenage boy once you know."

"That's why I'm worried."

"I'll talk to him. It'll be fine Kate."

"I hope so."

"Guess I need to pull out the shot gun!" Dad announces at the dinner table.

"Shotgun?"

"Don't look so horrified Kate. It's just an expression. I understand I'm meeting someone tomorrow night?"

I'm so wishing he didn't bring this up in front of Kelsey. Now, for sure, she'll be lingering around when Ryan arrives. "Yeah, Ryan Lambert. We are going to the movies tomorrow night." Then I add, "With a whole group."

"Your mom told me. By what time do I need to have my interrogation questions prepared?"

"Dad! Mom, I told you he will embarrass me." I am getting more uptight about this. My fingers beeline for my eyebrows and I start fiddling and tugging. This is not a habit I'm pleased to inherit.

"Kate, settle down. I'm just kidding."

"Okay. He's coming by around seven."

"Sounds good. Alyson, did you talk to her about curfew?"

"No. But I was thinking she comes home directly after the movie, and, by midnight."

Dad approves, "Works for me, how about you, Kate?"

"Fine by me." I hadn't really thought about curfew. But it seems reasonable, especially for my first date. Maybe this will go smoothly after all.

At 6PM a text comes through. "ON MY WAY. WALKING OVER. NO CAR."

I call him to ask, "What's going on?"

"Sorry, I couldn't get the car. My mom needs it to pick up

my sister from a birthday party. We can walk to the mall after I meet your parents."

"I can't walk all that way in the boots I have on," I explain.

"Can you change your shoes?"

"No, the outfit is set." Even I am surprised by my stubbornness.

He laughs, "It will have to be new shoes or a ride from your parents."

"Dang it. Well, my dad's a talker. You'll get an earful on the way to the mall."

"I can handle it. I'm almost there."

"K. Cool."

Nervous jitters as I wait for Ryan to arrive. I feel like it has been one set of jitters after the next since I received his original text. I need to get a hold of myself. This is a huge obstacle to surmount. The doorbell rings.

"Welcome," I say with a smile. "Come on in."

"Thanks." He saunters into the entry. Ryan doesn't seem nervous at all. My mom and dad are busying themselves by cleaning up from dinner. I expect Kelsey to slink in anytime.

"They are in the kitchen. Let's get this over with." For lack of a better word, by the time we enter, mom and dad are perched. Looking too eager, dad greets us.

"Come on in; Kate, who is your friend?" Like he doesn't know!

"Mom and Dad this is Ryan. Ryan, meet my parents, Joe and Alyson Malone."

"Hello, Mr. and Mrs. Malone." I think of Morgan. Will dad invite Ryan to call him Joe?

"Hi Ryan. Nice to meet you," mom starts.

"So, Ryan I understand you play lacrosse." Dad jumps right in.

"Yes, and some basketball, too," Ryan answers.

"Great, great. Tell me how lacrosse is going this year," dad continues. So far, so good but this is shaping up to be a long meet and greet.

"We are in 1st place but we haven't played M.I. yet. They'll be tough."

"That's always been a big rivalry; even when I played football for BHS." OMG, don't go there, dad! He continues, "Is Coach Phillips still there?" Oh, right, 40 years later!

"Yeah, he is! " Ryan confirms.

I start to wonder, is this for real?

"Wow. That's a career. I'm not surprised. That guy is really committed. In my time, he would show game film at his house and his wife would feed us pasta and garlic bread. It was insane. We took up the entire basement and she probably cooked for a weekend to feed all of us. I bet they'd never let a coach do that now."

"Probably not; but that's really cool," Ryan responds.

Mom steps in to hopefully wrap up the interview. "It seems that we have some mutual friends with your parents; the Bakers." Sounds like my mom did her homework.

"Yeah, my dad and Mr. Baker went to college together. We always spend 4th of July with them at their cabin."

"That sounds fun. We enjoy their company too; although, we haven't seen them for a while. I knew Sandy from work a long time ago. That is, before we "retired" to stay home with the kids." She laughs like that was funny or something.

"That's cool," Ryan says. The word count between my parents and Ryan is very lopsided. I'm sure he is weary. So, I step in, "Mom, Dad, we need to get to the mall, okay?"

"Mall? I thought you were headed to the movies?" mom asks.

"Oh yeah, we are going to the movies but we are meeting the crew at Yogurtland right before. It's in the mall."

"Sounds good," she concedes.

"But, oh!" I remember. "Can one of you give us a ride? Ryan walked over."

Dad replies, "I'll give you a ride. But, I do have one more question for Ryan."

"What?" I question him because he has that crafty, leprechaun look going on.

"Ryan, I was just wondering," he pauses briefly, "How do you feel about St. Patrick's Day?"

"Oh Dad!" I exclaim. Ryan looks puzzled. I interject, "Don't even answer. He's kidding."

"Yes I am! Had to make sure I embarrassed Kate." Dad is amused. "Let's get you to the mall!"

"Thanks, Mr. Malone," Ryan says. Dad doesn't correct the formality. That's interesting.

I can't get a word in during the ride. Dad and Ryan talk high school sports, college sports and professional sports for the entire 10 minute drive. They fit in more content than an ESPN segment. While I am glad the two are hitting it off, Dad's enthusiasm confirms my suspicions. He totally wishes he had a son.

The car pulls up to the curb and they are deep in conversation so I pipe in, "Hey you two catch the rest on SportsCenter tonight!"

"Alright, I'm coming. Thanks for the ride, Mr. Malone."

"No problem. But, Ryan?"

"Yeah?"

"Feel free to call me Joe."

"Cool."

I wouldn't call dad a pushover, but really, ten minutes of sports talk and Ryan is in the inner circle? Good news for me! "I'll call the house when the movie ends, K?"

"Sounds good, honey; have fun."

"Thanks Dad!"

Ryan squeezes my shoulder as we walk into the mall. "Your parents are really cool."

"They're alright, I guess."

"No really. Mine are strict and don't really talk to my friends about stuff that interests us."

"Like pasta feeds in the olden days?" I joke.

"That was cool! I bet your dad has some good stories."

"I bet he does too. But, I'm going to have to set a timer next time you come over to limit the sports talk!"

"Fair enough; but, I really do like your dad."

"Good. He likes you too. That's obvious." And then he squeezes my shoulder again, his signature move. And then, his face wraps around to greet mine. I smile and he kisses me.

I didn't expect it nor did I imagine the urgency of my response. I summon myself to return to my body as it is floating away in the delirium of my first kiss. His lips are so soft. Who knew? We pull away from each other and our eyes meet. We smile at each other and kiss again. I could do this all night! But, we can't.

Ryan says, "We better get to the yogurt place.. My phone is vibrating like crazy. They are stalking us."

"Okay," I feebly agree. I could bail on the movie altogether.

Our friends are assembled in the shop. No one has co-mingled yet. We each have a gazillion texts like, "WHERE R U?" A minute later, we enter the shop, and Ryan announces, "The social chairmen have arrived!" That breaks the ice.

We are finishing up our frozen yogurt when I see Carly walk by. She's alone. That's strange. Thank goodness Devyn isn't here. I don't need her to spoil my fun. And, it is a blast. Ryan's buddies are cool. A little gross with how they eat their yogurt but they can't help it. I glance over toward Madi and it looks like she might be flirting with the tall kid, Jack. They are sitting down so the height difference isn't so obvious. I can't wait for them to stand up. I am so busting Madi about this later!

Ryan the ringleader says, "Let's go. Movie is about to start."

I have takers so we head off. "Ryan, are you guys gonna get seats?" I ask.

"No, we'll hang here for you guys. Hurry though." He is especially accommodating. Funny what a first kiss can do.

"Okay. Let's go girls." We are giggling amongst ourselves. We all agree that the group thing is a fun option. Plus, Ryan's friends are making good impressions on the ladies. I couldn't be happier, in general. That's until I enter the restroom and catch eyes with Devyn and Carly washing their hands. I wonder if Carly saw all of us in Yogurtland. I'm about to find out.

"Hi you guys." I start.

Devyn surveys us. Maybe she thinks it's just us girls.

"Hi Kate, what are you seeing?"

"Avatar."

"Avatar? That's a weird choice when New Moon is out," she boldly states.

"Well, it's what the group wanted to see." I leave it at that. "Have fun," I add as I walk past them. I figure within seconds Devyn will put it all together when she sees the boy's right outside. Isn't there a saying about keeping your enemies close? I should remember that.

We file into the theatre. The gang disperses, as if abiding by an unwritten rule to leave Ryan and me on our own. We take the row behind the group Ryan gripping my hand as if I was walking a perilous cliff. While the girls and boys mixed and matched, I notice Madi sitting next to Ryan's buddy, Jack. Her head barely reaches his shoulder and I note to myself that regardless, it was probably best she didn't sit behind him if she wanted to see the screen. However, I'm thinking that her placement wasn't about seeing the movie. I consider whispering to her on our way by but Ryan's touch is coursing through my being and I just want to sit down and snuggle up.

"Look at our friends *getting to know each other….*" I lean in towards Ryan.

"I know. I don't think Jack has ever spoken to a girl alone until tonight and look at him, right next to Madi!" Ryan teases.

"Well, she certainly couldn't sit behind him if she wanted

to watch the movie at all!" with a giggle, I share my earlier thought.

"For sure" he laughs. "I'm not sure I need to watch the movie" he drapes his arm around my shoulder and my heart lurches.

I nestle into him, willing the darkness and noise to cloak us. I'm dying to kiss him again. As the lights dim I casually glance around the theatre looking at the neighboring audience. I don't recognize anyone, thank goodness. The coast is clear. Before the previews end, Ryan and I have picked up where we left off outside Yogurtland. We slump farther into our seats as our lips close in. I'm still a bit self-conscious and think about kissing as quietly as possible. And, it is possible to kiss and barely breathe and become one. We are totally in our own world. It's gentle and romantic and my body feels light as a feather. Then, the crashing sounds of the movie beginning bring us out of our singular state and Ryan finds my hand, smiles at me and redirects toward the opening scene.

I didn't really watch the movie, instead, I sat in bliss waiting for the next chance to snag a kiss. Avatar will go down as my favorite movie ever and not because I liked the story! Reluctantly, we leave the theatre.

Madi approaches and whispers, "Hey hot lips, want my mom to drop you off at home?"

Tease me all you want, I'm untouchable right now. "Sure, that'd be great. Spare me twenty questions from my dad" I say.

"Oh, we'll get plenty of questions from my mom as it is but at least I will be there to help you with the details from the movie" she teases again, but she's right.

"So true! I'll text my dad that I'll be home soon. Maybe they'll just go to bed."

"Hey, you should say goodnight to Ryan before my mom gets here". Madi has her A-game.

"Good thinking" as I peel away and find Ryan. "Night Ryan. That was a great movie, I think…" I smile and give him a peck on the lips.

"You can do better than that" he offers.

"I'd like to but not in the middle of this lobby. I have my reputation to protect" I say with lightheartedness.

"Whatever you say" he smiles and pecks me back and adds a bear hug whispering, "Talk to you tomorrow".

"Perfect" and I practically skip away.

Kelsey comes roaring into my room Sunday morning Announcing, "Kate, someone rolled our house! They must have used 100 rolls of toilet paper!"

"Oh my God, really?" I know exactly who it is. Brutus.

"Dad is out there right now cleaning it up. Mom and dad laughed a little bit until they realized what a mess it is."

"Is there any sign of who did it?" I ask.

"Not that I can tell."

"Oh. I'll be right out."

"I'll tell dad." Kelsey says as she scoots out of my room.

Kelsey is right. It is a huge mess. Thankfully it didn't rain last night but there is enough moisture to make it a laborious clean up. "Oh wow," I say.

Dad agrees, "Yep. That's for sure. This reeks of meanness not fun. So, Kate, did anything happen at the movies last night?"

"No, nothing at all." This statement is true because nothing "happened" I just happened to be with Ryan and Devyn didn't like it.

"Well, there was a message attached to this mess. I picked it up before your mom or Kelsey came out," he says.

"What?" I say with a pit in my stomach. Hurry dad, spit it out.

"In toilet paper on the grass, 'Kate Sucks' was spelled out."

"Oh my God… it's Devyn. I knew it."

"What happened?" he asks.

"I saw her in the bathroom before the movie. Then, she

walked out to see Ryan and his buddies. She probably put it together that we were hanging out and got mad."

"I may never understand girls," dad suggests.

"Me neither," I add for a bit of levity.

"Kate, you should take care of this rivalry. This is malicious," dad warns.

"I know. She's always had it out for me and I have never understood why."

"Why don't you ask her?"

"Oh Dad; I usually just ignore her."

"It's not working anymore."

"I'm not sure anything will work," I insist.

"I suggest you find out. I don't want to spend my Sunday mornings filling up our recycle bin with toilet paper."

"No doubt."

"Get some shoes on and come help me before all the neighbors start nosing around."

"K."

Holed up in my bedroom, I finally get through to Ryan. "Where have you been? I've been stalking you all day."

"I noticed! I had a lacrosse tournament," he says.

"I would've come."

"I would have liked you to but I haven't exactly told my parents about you yet."

"Who's keeping secrets now?" I tease.

"I know, I know. I told you my parents are pretty strict. They've never encouraged me to have a girlfriend. They think you, I mean, any girlfriend is too distracting."

"Distracting from school?"

"Yeah. School and lacrosse."

"What, so are you trying to go pro or something?" I ask.

"No, but some help with college would be good."

"Got it. Well, figure it out soon. I'd like to watch you play on your club team."

"Bossy!"

I laugh, then remember my morning and say, "Ryan, you're never gonna believe this."

"What?"

"Devyn and at least a few others covered my front yard in toilet paper last night."

"You got rolled?"

"Yes. Like about 100 rolls. It took up our whole recycle can."

"How do you know it was Devyn?"

"She and I aren't exactly buddies and she saw you and me together at the movies last night."

"So?"

"Dummy, everyone knows she likes you! Plus, she wrote 'Kate Sucks' in t-p on the lawn."

"Girls!" he laughs.

"It's not 'girls', it's her! She's crazy," I say.

"What are you gonna do?"

"My dad thinks I need to say something. This one-sided rivalry has been going on since 7th grade."

"Good luck with that."

"Geez, thanks for the support."

"I'll be there to pick up the pieces. Make sure you do it in a public place."

"You are not helping!"

"Okay, sorry. So, you deal with Devyn and then we can hang out? Need to go to tutorial again? Wink—wink?" Ryan jokes. "I better come clean with my mom" he pauses and gives our next encounter some thought. "Maybe we could take Ashley to a park? I'm sure my mom would go for that." He adds, "Ashely too for that matter. She's getting way more attention with you around."

I reply, "Good plan; she you in the morning!" In all its glory, my clover tree presides above me. I sit up and put my hand over my most recent clover labeled, BOYFRIEND and fill my heart with all the gratitude I can muster. With perfect timing, my clover tree produced my most favorite wish so far!

I feel nauseous walking into the lunch room. Like a laser beam, I see Devyn already at the lunchtable. It's time to confront the enemy. With all my willpower, I decide to march over confidently, sit down and get the words out fast.

It's difficult, but I look right at her and say, "Nice artwork in my yard over the weekend." I take a deep breath. "What's your problem with me?"

"No problem," she quickly rebukes.

I'm shaking but I don't think she can tell plus, I'm committed so I say, "Clearly you do. You have since Jr. High."

"Kate, you prance around like a princess; like you don't care about anyone else's opinion," Devyn says.

"That's not true. I value other people's opinions."

"Not mine."

"You have never been a good friend to me, Devyn."

"I've tried to get your attention. But, you never try back."

"Devyn, you try too hard and I just never thought you liked me very much."

"Kate, you just get everything you want. Like, Ryan."

"I don't see it that way. I work really hard for things. And Ryan, well, that was unexpected. But I'm not complaining. I like him a lot."

"Whatever," Devyn retorts. Darn it, I thought we were making headway.

"This isn't going anywhere. But, I need a truce. My parents were not happy about the toilet paper and it was obvious who did it."

"Fine, truce," Devyn offers with a snide look on her face.

Wishing I had eyes on the back of my head, I walk away. I'm

sure this agreement is about as legitimate as Brutus agreeing to a truce with Julius Caesar.

"I haven't been on a swing in *soooo* long!" I exclaim. Ashley is next to me pumping her little legs as hard as she can to get some elevation but I'm already soaring. It's the simplest of pleasures, swinging. I am giggling like I'm six years old myself. Ashley begs for help, "Ryan, please push me. I'm hardly moving."

He meanders over and gives her a big push, running right under her chair, "Underdog!"

"My dad used to say that to us!" I remark as Ashley giggles. The childhood memories are flooding in.

Ryan circles back around to torment me. As my swing brings me closer to the ground, he swats my bottom and I squeal with delight. "Stop it!" But of course I want him to continue. So, I escalate my leg pumping to swing even higher, his fingertips can barely reach me and then, down again. A playful, whap! "Ryan!" He moves back over to Ashley to give her some momentum. "Hey, I want a turn," he says sounding like a school boy himself..

Meanwhile, I am swinging so high I'm practically parallel to the top bar. And in that moment when the swing pauses before it heads back down, time seems to stop. I take it all in. The sheer joy of their companionship, the sun on my face, the fresh air; it's the way I want to feel all the time. As if this new revelation was enough closure, I generously offer up my swing and leisurely find a place on the grass. After a few minutes of bonding with his sister, Ryan joins me.

"Ashley looks like she could swing all day," I say.

Ryan pulls off his Notre Dame sweatshirt and folds it up into a pillow and sets it on my lap. In one movement he lays down beside me with his head on the pillow looking toward me and the blue sky. As if I know what I'm doing, I smile down at him and run my fingers through his hair. It's the most intimate moment I've ever had and my fondness for him seems to be reciprocal.

Ryan closes his eyes.

"I could fall asleep," he admits.

"I know; the sun on my face is making me drowsy too."

"I'm just tired. I never get to lie around like this. I have four lacrosse games this week" he sighs.

I glance down, "I'm hanging out with the cutest and busiest boy in school." He smiles drowsily. I add, "I only have one soccer game this week. We've gotta win though." I stop myself. "But I don't want to think about that right now. This moment in time is perfect." We comfortably sit in silence. Until the silence is broken by Ashley teasing, "Ryan has a girlfriend! Ryan has a girlfriend!"

His eyes open and he gazes fondly at me, "I guess I do."

Winning eluded us despite our renewed faith in Coach Kelly and our hard work. As the losses piled up, I had to re-define success. Ryan helped me through my frustration.

"A 2-6 record; that sucks," I complain.

"It sucks to lose, but at least the team is improving," he offers.

"That's easy for you to say, your team is still alive in State."

"We were terrible last year though," Ryan says. "In the end, I had fun anyway."

"You sound like my dad. He is always looking for silver linings."

"I'm just thinking that there are other things about the season that you can salvage; like, how fun it is to play for BHS."

"Especially in the stadium under the lights—that's fun," I add.

"Exactly!"

"And, you're right, we are improving."

"See?"

"Yeah, I get it."

Ryan feels like he succeeded in his pep talk which results in a congratulatory hug and some kisses which would have fixed everything in the first place.

CHAPTER SIXTEEN

By all accounts, it seems like Ryan's parents like me. I've joined them for dinner a few times and of course, we exchange pleasantries at all of Ryan's lacrosse games. But, they seem real intent on keeping him too busy for a girlfriend. We do our best to see each other outside of school but they really have him reined in and very scheduled. Ryan mentioned that he feels exasperated by it sometimes but he knows how much they need him to get an athletic scholarship if he wants to go to college. He figures I understand since soccer is so important to me, but honestly, I wish we could carve out more time together.

Tonight we are meeting at the athletic club. We usually shoot hoops or play racquetball. I think he likes that I'm competitive and really try to beat him. I'm going to lobby for a racquetball game; I'm feeling the win tonight. I gather up my things and check in with my parents before I leave.

Mom quizzes me, "So, you are going to the club?"

"Yep. Can I have a ride? Ryan is meeting me there straight from practice."

"Sure but I want you home by 10PM, okay?"

"Okay."

"Homework done?"

"Yep."

Dad pipes in, "Say, how is Ryan's lacrosse team doing?"

"They are in second, behind MI," I reply.

"When do they match up?"

"I can't remember. Soon, I think. I'll ask him tonight."

"Why don't you have Ryan come by here and pick you up next time you guys go out?" dad suggests. "I'd like to see him again and catch up with BHS sports."

"Will do."

"I like that kid. Have fun. Kick some butt."

I giggle, "I will!"

It's impossible to roam the club without running into at least one of my parents' friends. Whoever it is, they always make a point to say hello. I know it's their way of sending the message that, "You have been sighted." I'm sure my parents do the same to other kids. We swipe our membership cards when we enter but we could easily march right out and go somewhere else. While the club's security system seems flimsy, the "you have been sighted" system the adults use is appears to be airtight. But, that doesn't mean I have to engage them all in a conversation. When I am solo I can walk through the halls with my head hung low or pretend I'm texting in order to avoid eye contact. But, today I have Ryan at my side and I see Mr. Murphy right away. I can't avoid him; he's one of my dad's good friends. I wonder if he was planted by my dad to keep tabs. We are moving briskly toward the racquetball courts but there is no way I can pretend not to see Mr. Murphy. I'm proactive and say, "Hi, Mr. Murphy."

Mr. Murphy doesn't know Ryan and I don't want to stop and introduce him.

"Well, Kate Malone. How are you?"

I'm still walking fast, but Ryan slows down. He is so flipping polite! "I'm good. How are you?" I'm forced to stop.

"Fine, just fine. I'm heading over to Sun Valley next week," Mr. Murphy says.

"That sounds fun." I obliging reply. We are all staring at each other, so I take the lead and say, "Mr. Murphy, this is Ryan Lambert."

"Hi Ryan, it's nice to meet you."

His response is respectful and genuine. "It's nice to meet you too." At least he's making a good impression.

"Well, we have a racquetball court reserved. Have a safe drive to Sun Valley!" I say. Ryan whispers, "What's the big hurry?"

"I'm not in the mood to chit chat. I'm glad we are playing racquetball so we are sequestered from everyone we know."

"I'm flattered you want me all to yourself," says Ryan nudging me.

"Enjoy it while you can because your ego is about to take a hit," I tease.

"Well, okay. Bring it on!" I get the feeling he isn't quite sure what to do with me.

We enter the court and Ryan clearly doesn't understand the gravity of the competition yet. He keeps flirting with me, but I'm not engaging. Of course, I love it, but, the crazy competitor side of me is in full swing. I start to understand that I have a secondary advantage. Let's see how long it takes him to understand that I am in competition mode.

A few serves into it and already Ryan tries to sweet talk his way out of it. "Kate, you look so pretty tonight." Wait until you see me sweat off my make up! Then he adds more, "I love when you pull your hair back."

"I pulled it back so it wouldn't get in my way while I beat you!"

The points ratchet up for both of us; it's close. "This isn't how I expected this to go. Way too close for comfort," Ryan admits. I smile. Obviously, he hasn't dated anyone like me before. I hope this doesn't go sideways but I can't help myself.

It's a good game. Thank goodness I'm more competitive than vain because sweat is dripping down my face and back. I'm sure I don't look "cute" at all. I wonder if he would rather be up in the weight room "showing me how to lift weights" while I look on adoringly in my sassy workout clothes. He seems satisfied with his girlfriend offering up some good, healthy competition instead. I wonder if losing to his competitive girlfriend will be okay. We'll see!

I can tell he is starting to panic as I stay in the game. Ryan is playing hard without pulling away in points so he attempts to sabotage my momentum. He brings on the charm.

"Kate, you look thirsty. Let's take a *water break.*" The tone of his voice illustrates his motive. As much as water and a possible kiss from Ryan tempt me, I do not relent.

"Good try," I reply. "We just had a break. Game on!"

I squeak out a last minute victory as he botches the game point return. I'm as gracious as I can be while I jump up and down in victory! He walks over to me and offers me his hand in a gesture of congratulations. His hand?

And, as I reach across he grabs me and nestles me to his chest. There is no victory handshake; Ryan kisses me through all my lingering sweat!

"Great game Kate; you are awesome. But, I want a rematch soon."

"Thanks Ry. Rematch anytime," I say as I kiss him back. I have the best boyfriend in the whole world!

CHAPTER SEVENTEEN

Not much can dampen my spirits these days. Ryan and I are hangin' out whenever we can so everything is good. That's why I feel so blindsided by Sara's announcement on the bus ride home, "I'm not trying out for Premier soccer this year Kate." She adds, "I'm just not feeling it."

I'm shocked. "What, why?"

"I'm considering trying other things."

"Like what?" I ask incredulously

"Lacrosse looks fun."

"Well, yeah, if you started like, when you were ten. Those teams are as solid as our soccer team. You know the drill; someone basically needs to lose a spot, for you to win it."

She gets defensive, "Well Kate, I don't know. Maybe not lacrosse. Maybe not anything!"

"Sara, do your parents know about this decision?"

" I told them this morning and I don't think they believe me since tryouts are tonight."

I added, "I don't believe it either! We need you. I need you! You are part of the team. I don't understand!"

"Kate, you know I didn't get much playing time during the high school season. I don't think I can risk not making the Premier team."

"Sara, that was weird. Coach just kept moving you around

from position to position. You did great; she just never gave you a permanent position. You know you have a place on the Premier team, right?"

"I'm not certain Kate. I'm nervous. I know Coach Tom attended a lot of our high school games. He likely noticed I played all over the place. Who knows what he thinks?"

"You can decide *for* him or come out and try out with all of us. You know tryouts are just a formality. We've been together for so long," I say with conviction.

"Alright, I'll go."

"Sweet—my mom can probably drive."

"Okay. I'll be ready."

I add, "Sara…."

"What?" she asks.

"Be confident. Visualize the player you want to be tonight, okay?" As the words come out, I know I sound like my dad; feels strange.

"K. See you tonight. And thanks!"

I wasn't nervous at Premier tryouts this year but maybe I should have been. Our team has been together for a few years but when the results came out, there is total upheaval. No one saw it coming; at least I know I certainly didn't. The call came in as usual, right around dinner time. I gladly accepted my spot on the team, assuming this was happening right down the roster of last year's squad. I figured Coach would pick up a girl to fill our one void but who knew?

Shortly after my acceptance call, the phone rang again. The caller ID reads, BRANDON, ROBERT. It's Madi! So I answer.

"Hi Madi!" Before I can launch into self congratulatory screams with her, she interrupts me.

"Kate, Coach just called me." She doesn't sound right.

"Yeah, me too!" I interject, trying to change the inflection.

"But, he told me…" and her voice drifts and catches some emotion, "that I would be offered a spot on the B team this year." And she starts to cry—a lot.

"Oh no!" I exclaim. A mixture of disbelief, compassion and anger is taking form.

She is crying inconsolably. I try to comfort her, "Madi, I am so sorry. It could be because of your injury. Maybe he just wants to give you a chance to get your hip healthy again? And then most likely you will get more playing time."

Through the tears, "Yeah, that's what my mom said. My parents are pretty upset too. This isn't how we expected the night to go, ya know."

"Me neither! Omigosh."

"Well, my mom and dad are trying to make me feel better with some dessert. I better go before I start crying again. I'm really bummed, ya know. I'll miss everyone."

I am starting to feel like crying so I quickly say, "I'll miss you too. But, I get to see you at school every day!" It is a feeble attempt to soothe her but I hope it helps.

"Yeah, that's good. See you tomorrow."

"Bye."

I hang up the phone, crushed. My parents and now Kelsey are eyeing me wondering what the heck is going on.

Kelsey starts, "Who was that?"

"Madi."

"What happened?" in chorus.

My eyes well up at the sadness of it all. These things matter a lot when you are 15.

"Madi was cut from our team!"

My parents don't seem as stunned as me but they offer their condolences; mostly because they understand the magnitude of our friendship. "I'm sorry Kate" my mom said first. "It will be strange not having Madi on the team. But, you two are such good friends; we will make sure your friendship stays intact."

Dad sat quietly, gently tugging on his eyebrows, taking it all in before he spoke, "You know me and my silver linings. This could be a great move for her. She can regain her health, confidence and quite possibly be a leader on her new team."

"I guess," I said. It's hard to look at the positives while I know one of my best friends is at home, hurting. I drag myself back into my room and write Madi a note. I pull out a bag of Sour Patch Kids from the "candy stash" my mom doesn't know about and wrap the card and a ribbon around them to give to Madi tomorrow.

Recently, I moved the clover tree to the back of my bedroom door. It catches my eye. One of the clovers, which is now dry and brittle, needs some more glue. I look at it closely. It is hanging from one of the older branches of my tree. One of my original hopes and dreams, MAKE THE PREMIER SOCCER TEAM, has been laying the foundation for years of additional wishes for me. I thought about Madi and whether at some point she started doubting herself as an A team player. Was there a time that the mere suggestion that she wouldn't make it, infiltrated her thoughts? I think about how I marched into tryouts as confident as ever. Since the moment I made that team two years ago, I have never visualized myself anywhere else. I contemplate it all for a moment and label another clover, MADI HAS A GREAT SOCCER SEASON ON HER NEW TEAM. I imagine her as a confident team leader. She is smiling. Our lunchtime conversations are reciprocal stories of success. She believes it is the best thing that happened to her. I believe it for her and with her as it runs through my mind. It's the most I can do for my friend right now.

Any stillness our suburban neighborhood enjoys is interrupted when Janie's mom drives carpool. The weekly rite of passage is to endure the blaring sounds of *"We got more bounce in California*

than all yours combined. We got more bounce in California; we like to party all the time!"

Janie announces her arrival with a signature song. Which I do find catchy, but really, doesn't she realize she lives in Washington now?

Janie's mom pulls into the driveway. I am ready and waiting. The song is not over so I'm happy to enjoy it. When it ends, I am compelled to ask Sara, "Does she do that to you too?"

"Yes, and elderly neighbors next door were weeding today and most certainly they rolled their eyes!"

Janie and her mom lock eyes and giggle.

Those Californians ruffle our feathers!

The rhythm of our soccer carpool falls into place, less one. We miss Madi but Janie has some seriously high energy. We complain about school, teachers, goofy kids in our classes. Then, as if she's the social chairman of our ride, Janie offers up a riddle: "So, there's an electric train that travels on many different tracks. One day it heads south and turns east. Another day it heads west and turns north. Today, the train heads north only. What direction is the smoke from the stack headed?"

We clamor.

"Is the train moving?" I probe

"Yes," Janie says

Sara throws an answer out there, "Its moving south, and the opposite direction of the train!"

"Yes!" I say.

And then Janie giggles and says, "Nope."

We suffer in silence since we can't come up with another answer quickly. We demand Janie tell us the answer,

"It's an electric train! There's no smoke!"

"*Ahhhhhh,*" Sara and I collectively sigh.

"Okay, I have another," says Janie and she starts, "So there is a man that lives on the 9th floor of a building…."

Even though I am fully enjoying the brain teasers, my mind wanders. I think that some of the other girls from school would probably make fun of us sharing "riddles". They are too cool for such silliness. They are always trying out more mature topics to impress each other. But, we are far away from the high school campus and all of us are eager to participate in the riddle storytelling and solving!

Janie continues on with the riddle, "Every clear day the man rides the elevator down if there are other passengers and takes the stairs up to his apartment on the 9th floor after work. On rainy days he rides the elevator both ways. Why?"

We scramble for answers.

I say, "Because the elevator is outdoors and he needs his umbrella!"

I know it doesn't make sense, but it's all I have. Sara is a "ponderer" and keeps pondering....

Mrs. Bennett says, "On rainy days the stairwell is closed!"

"Nope," says Janie with a smile.

Sara says, "He feels more energetic on clear days, which encourages him to take the stairs."

That is *soooo* Sara!

"Nope," repeats Janie.

When Mrs. Bennett announces that we are at the exit for practice, we beg Janie to tell us the answer!

She complies, "He is a dwarf!"

Her mom interjects, "Hey, he's a *small person*."

"Okay, yeah, he's a small person and he needs the umbrella to reach the 9th floor button on the elevator!" Janie explains.

"*Ahhhh,*" we all get it simultaneously.

We giggle at the silliness of the riddle and gather our stuff for practice.

This is what I love about my soccer friends. There is no jockeying to "fit in". By virtue of making the team, we have a place and an instant group to call our own. We can goof around and be silly. And, as my mom says, "Act our age."

CHAPTER EIGHTEEN

I march into Kelsey's room certain that she borrowed the scarf I want to wear today. I thrust open her closet door ready to rummage when something catches my eye. To my surprise, Kelsey's very own clover tree is presenting itself to me in all of its abundance! My first reaction is a slight betrayal from my dad. When did he take Kelsey to the clover field? And, did she sit under his desk writing stories too? I thought the clover tree was our special secret. But, the voice of reason chimes in that, of course, he would share it with my sister as well.

After the wave of annoyance that I have to share the magic passes, I begin to feel a bit sneaky. Here are many of Kelsey's hopes and dreams staring right at me! I can't help it; I'm compelled to check it out. I start taking in the hopes and dreams that drape the branches of her clover tree. I look at the older ones: NEW ACRYLICS, DESK FOR MY ROOM, and HARMONY. Harmony? I wonder what she meant by that; and, did she get it? There are a dozen others on the tree, several of which I can confirm came true. I take a risk and find one clover that looks newly labeled. WIN ART COMPETITION. I'm excited for her and for us. We can work together manifesting wishes. I'm thinking we should start with, TRIP TO HAWAII!

I hustle out of the house, and run to the bus stop. "Darn it!" I mutter. I never found the scarf. My outfit is incomplete!

It's sinking in that the clover tree is not just mine. I had put it back in the "metaphorical" vault after the sleepover debacle in 7th grade and have kept it to myself ever since. I've had moments where I've felt a bit selfish, hoarding this prized knowledge but it seemed better than ridicule. Now today, my sister's clover tree reveals itself and to compound it all, Madi joins us with her news at lunch.

"I was named Team Captain!" she says proudly at lunch.

"That's awesome!" I answer right away as I am truly happy for her.

Sara is equally relieved and excited with the news, "Oh, Madi, what a great honor. Congratulations!"

"Yeah," she adds, "I've really felt like a leader. It's different than our old team; I'm way more confident. Less pressure, I guess. But anyway, the team voted, not the coach, and they picked me!"

"You rock girl!" I say.

And then it comes crashing in, the clover tree worked its magic on Madi! I can use it for the benefit of others too! The energy shift with this revelation is surreal. I'm even more empowered than before. The clover tree is so powerful. I am in awe.

The bus approaches my stop and I notice my sister walking up the street. Our school ends an hour later than hers and she is just getting home. I wonder what's up with her.

I lumber off the bus. Dang, this backpack is heavy. I catch up to my sister and ask, "Kelsey, why are you walking home so late?"

"Oh, I am taking an art class after school. I really like it."

"That's cool." I'm mildly interested but I mostly wanted to know if she got in trouble or something. Her answer verifies that she is not in trouble.

And then I remember the clover tree and my scarf! "Kelsey, I was looking for my scarf this morning. Do you have it?"

"Oh, yeah, it is hanging off the back of my desk chair." She starts to apologize because normally not returning a borrowed item would elicit a much more negative response from me. But I stop her with my next question, "I noticed your clover tree in your closet."

"Yeah, daddy taught me all about the clover field last summer."

"That's cool. Sorry, I couldn't help but look. I notice you have a lot of clovers already."

"Oh, that's okay. I just put it in my closet because daddy kind of thought I should keep it to myself for a while. You know, not share it with my friends just yet." I instantly remembered my own lesson in keeping the clover sacred and said, "Yeah, that's a good idea."

"I do have a lot of clovers. My own clover tree like yours! I like it because it makes me really think about the things I want for myself. Before, I just asked for things at Christmastime or wanted the cool stuff my friends had. Now, I really sit down and consider my hopes and dreams. My friends would never really get it anyway. It took daddy a few times to teach it to me!"

"That's awesome Kelse. We should put our clover energies together sometime and get ourselves a family trip to Hawaii or a ski boat!"

"For sure!"

"Mom would be so happy to see us cooperating!" I say with confidence.

CHAPTER NINETEEN

Ryan isn't at my locker this morning so I shoot off a text, "R U AT SCHOOL YET?" He replies, "IN THE LIBRARY."

"K. BE RIGHT THERE."

I beeline right toward him to take advantage of the few minutes before the bell rings.

"Hey!" I say. I'm always excited to see him.

"Hey there," he says, lacking enthusiasm.

"Should we go to the arcade this weekend?" I ask.

"Can't, my grandparents are coming into town."

"Again?"

"Yeah. And, we have to do family photos or something like that."

"Well, you wanna hang out after school for a little bit?"

"I have to get my hair cut. You know, for the family photos."

"Got it." This has been the trend for a few weeks now and it feels like I'm in an uphill battle to get face time with Ryan. So I am going to pout. "Well, let me know when you are available," I say as I stomp off.

It doesn't feel right to stomp off but I'm so frustrated. I'm trying to get a point across since nothing else has worked lately. He doesn't chase after me, so apparently, this tactic didn't work either.

It felt more like a gradual drifting apart than a break up. Months of, "I have lacrosse practice or a family barbeque or I'm hangin with my buddies" and there was never time for me. I still got off the bus, anticipating our reunion at the lockers but the ritual went by the wayside. I asked him about it and I could hear the frustration in his answer, "Kate, I get home from lacrosse at 9PM and then I need to eat real quickly and I'm up really late doing homework. I've been sleeping in and barely make the bell."

Earlier in the week, I resorted to calling his house and speaking with his mom, who is polite but distant. It took all of my nerve to even pick up the phone and she has to be short with me! Geez. "Hi, Mrs. Lambert, it's Kate. Is Ryan home?"

"No, Ryan's not available. I'll tell him you called." *Hmmm*, not available or not home?

I'm convinced the dissolution was orchestrated by Ryan's parents. I liken it to classic brainwashing. No time for a girlfriend, but there's plenty of time for him to execute their plan for him. I wonder if there's a place where their dream for him ends, and his dream for himself starts.

Yet, they don't shoulder all the blame, the final blow was executed by Ryan himself. It started with a text: "HEY. YOU CALLED THE HOUSE. I'M NEVER THERE EXCEPT TO SLEEP. REALLY BUSY WITH LACROSSE AND REF CLASS. MEET ME AFTER SCHOOL TOMORROW AT THE LOCKERS." Ref class? But, I'm hopeful in my reply, "UR HOUSE?"

"NO. JUST REAL QUICKLY AFTER SCHOOL. K?"

Not feeling confident anymore, "K. CAN'T MISS THE BUS THO."

"K."

He starts with, "Hey." Ryan seems nervous so I get a pit in my stomach.

"Hi." I should be bracing myself but I don't.

Maybe I shouldn't have told him about not missing the bus because his words are rushed and blunt. "We need to take a break. I don't have time." I am speechless. He keeps talking, "It's just that I'm so busy. Now my mom wants me to ref so I can help with the lacrosse expenses. I have that stupid class plus lacrosse and school."

Exasperation and heartbreak are my primary emotions. It's all I can do to stay composed and not burst into tears. Somehow I muster the words, "I had fun."

"Yeah, me too; you are a really cool girl," he offers.

"Apparently not cool enough to rank above everything else." I reply sarcastically.

"It's not like that."

"Yes, it is. I gotta go." I really want the last word for some reason.

"I think you missed the bus."

"I'll just walk home."

"Want me to walk you home?"

"No. But, I'm sure you don't have time anyway."

"I guess you're right. I need to get home."

"Right," I say. He leans over and hugs me which makes it worse. I turn on my heels and walk away before he sees my eyes welling up with tears.

My phone ringing helps me realize I'm already halfway home.

It's my mom. "Kate, where are you? You are late."

"Oh, sorry Mom; I missed the bus."

"Why didn't you call me? I could have picked you up."

"I wanted to walk. Ryan and I broke up today after school."

"Oh sweetie, I'm sorry. That really hurts, huh?"

"Yeah, I'm really sad. I'm almost home."

"Okay. We can talk about it when you get home," mom suggests.

"Maybe."

"Whatever works for you, sweetie. But, call if you want me to come get you."

On the homestretch of my walk I wonder if I could have been a better girlfriend and held a place higher on his "to do list". My mind races; should I have been more "needy", less independent and competitive? Or, "girly". Perhaps I should wear more make up and not let him see me sweat? Or, "intimate"? I've heard of all the girls that have given up themselves for their boyfriends. From what I can tell, it's risky business. None of my questions about our relationship resonate. Not with Ryan. He's not like that. So, maybe I should have been more demanding of his time? No, it would have ended sooner if I became another obligation for him. Basically Ryan is not the director of his own movie. I feel some compassion mixed in with my sadness. But, by the time I get home, I feel desperate that it is over. I lost Ryan. My 15 minutes of fame turned into a few months. It will take some time to recover.

"I'll be in my room," I say to my mom. She gives me a hug. I'm glad she is home for moral support. I plop down on my bed and look over at my clover tree. I say aloud, "Well, I didn't know this clover tree wish had an expiration date." But, it did and I am heartbroken. Taylor Swift is right, *"When you're fifteen and somebody tells you they love you/ you're gonna believe them…."*

I drift off to sleep exhausted from heartbreak. I awake to a knock on my bedroom door.

"Come in." It's Morgan.

"Hey, Morgan."

"Your mom told me when I called. So I came over. I'm sorry."

"It sucks." My word choice reflects my mood.

"Totally sucks. What happened? But only if you want to tell me, of course." Morgan is so considerate.

I tell her the official "breakup story" without crying because after some thought; part of me feels like it could have been worse. Morgan agrees. "I believe him when he says he's just too busy, don't you?" she asks.

"Yeah, I guess I do. Still…."

"Kate, I bet that was really hard for him to do. And at least he's not like that tool, Dylan, who broke up with his girlfriend by text."

"Oh, that would have been horrible!" I admit. "And, humiliating" I add.

"Ryan's not like that" she reminds me.

"I know. I'm still sad."

"For now." Morgan's confidence in my future his helpful.

The vultures, namely Devyn, don't take long to attack. By the end of the week, she asked Ryan to the Spring TOLO dance. It's the only dance of the year that the girls are supposed to initiate the date. And, the creativity and oftentimes theatrics that accompany the invitations are better than the event itself! The lunchtime buzz is that she sent a lacrosse stick to his house with the words, "TOLO with Devyn, It starts at 7. Wear cowboy boots, it'll be a hoot." What a lame rhyme. Best of all, I heard he declined. I bet his mom was behind it. She probably has him booked out already. Or, his grandparents are in town again! I laugh. I haven't laughed all week. It feels good.

Sara brings up the subject, "Are you considering someone to invite to TOLO?"

"No, I'm not in the mood. Couldn't Ryan have waited until after TOLO? I really wanted to go."

"I know, poor timing."

"Are you gonna ask someone, Sara?"

"I'm considering asking Sean, that boy in my Science class," she says.

"You've been talking about him a lot! You should!" I exclaim.

"I was hoping to double date. Can I persuade you otherwise?"

"No, it's too soon. I'd be terrible company. Ask Madi if she wants to go."

"I will. But, I know there are numerous boys that would love to attend with you."

"That's nice, Sara. But, I'm out."

Part III

GRADE 11

Chapter Twenty

With an academic tone, I proclaim at breakfast, "Summer slipped by like water through a sieve."

My sister grunts, "Whatever." And even my mom rolls her eyes. These days, I notice that she may be rolling her eyes at me almost as much as I do it to her. Our summer writing assignment focused on "analogies" and I can't help but incorporate them into my daily observations. It is driving my mom crazy. But, hey, I'm 16; it's my job to drive my mom crazy.

But, the summer did go by too fast. Janie was away at soccer camp in California for like, a month. Morgan had relatives in and out for weeks and Madi and Sara took a bunch of family trips. So, the end of summer brings a much anticipated reunion with my buddies; and, a jarful of clovers to mark the beginning of a new school year.

The clovers greet me and I know exactly what I will wish for this year! I plop down on my bed and begin to visualize the State Cup Championship. State Cup isn't until spring but dad likes us to set our goals for the year. Amongst other hopes and dreams I jot down for myself, the State Cup Championship is a realistic opportunity and dream of mine since I made the team in 7th grade. Our Premier team is touted to win but we've had such hopes of winning State before. So, this year I paint a picture unlike a State Cup I've experienced in the past. I imagine myself dribbling down the field. The turf pellets stream behind me as I cut toward the goal. I thread a pass through to Janie, whose ball skills send her and the ball right by the defender. Abbey is there to help but Janie doesn't need her for this one, low shot into the corner! And so it goes. Unlike previous years, we pound the goal and take a healthy lead in the game. Madi and Sara are tight in the back for a shutout. The energy in the stands feels like a big football game. It is electric! I'm working hard on the field and feeling parched. The feeling is so real that I take a sip of my water sitting on my bedside table. As my visualization continues I remember to feel grateful for the healthy body that helps me play, the competitive mind that keeps me engaged and the joy I feel out on the pitch vying for a title! Our success fills every cell of my body. And finally, I deem a fresh clover, "2009 State Cup Soccer Championship". I carve out a few more minutes to add some more clovers to the tree. I hastily add the High School 3A Soccer championship. After three years, Coach Kelly has put together a pretty good squad. I feel good about my effort. I'm armed and ready for school to start!

CHAPTER TWENTY ONE

Junior year and specifically Honors English is turning out to be killer. I love my teacher even though she isn't very likable. Ms. Harrington is a large woman with wild hair. She walked in the first day of school and proclaimed, "I am agnostic." I guess her proclamation is relevant because she proceeded to hand out the syllabus and the first text listed was the *Scofield Reference Bible, Authorized King James Version*. Hallelujah! I guess.

Mrs. Harrington really lured the class into liking her with interesting curriculum. We read Conrad, Kafka and Shakespeare and compare themes throughout the Bible. New terms like allegory, protagonist and motif fill my brain. It is fascinating making connections. The curriculum Mrs. Harrington proposes is a surprising twist coming from a self proclaimed agnostic. But, I guess she doesn't have a conflict of interest! As I am not a regular churchgoer, it is my first experience with the Bible. Mrs. Harrington expertly navigates us through the rich and cumbersome text. I find the parallels fascinating and so do my classmates. Before we know it, we are proving her theory that "every work of literature is derived from the Bible". Mrs. Harrington goes so far as to deem Shakespeare the original "Soap Opera writer" and to our delight, we spend an entire class watching soaps and sifting through *The Complete Works of Shakespeare*. The soap opera we watched had some serious parallels to *Hamlet*, "Neither a borrower nor a lender be; For loan oft loses both itself and friend, and borrowing dulls the edge of husbandry." (Act I, Sc. III) OMG.

Our work with the bible continues. *Paradise Lost* by Milton is our current epic. But, today we are studying symbolism in all the works we've read. Mrs. Harrington revisits the symbol of the rooster or "cock". Our class can barely contain itself. She insists we keep taking notes.

"The cock," she says, "symbolizes the 'imprisoned spirit', 'pride and defiance', 'sexual drive', 'dominance'. The cock breaks free so it can realize his life force."

Madi reaches over and writes in my notebook, "I think Mrs. H is a nympho". LMAO!

And in a defining moment as an AP English teacher, Mrs. Harrington says, "The cock represents liberation of passion." TMI!

I made the leap of faith that liking the curriculum and liking the teacher should go together. It wasn't long before Mrs. Harrington revealed herself to me and nearly toppled a belief system I held dearly.

It all started with a simple request. Just a few months into the year, Mrs. Harrington broached the subject of college entrance applications. She knew that most of the Honors class would apply to four year universities, and she wanted us to write our college admissions essay as a class assignment. Naturally, part of the process was to disclose our university of choice. I was pleased to get this albatross of an assignment off my back and ultimately end up with a great essay to submit. It was arduous and required a lot of introspection, but I was pleased with my final product. Mrs. Harrington offered us unlimited rewrites until we got it right so I wasn't discouraged at the first wave of comments relating to the letter, "You need more 'voice', let them 'hear' Kate in this letter."

"Don't make this a laundry list of your accomplishments. Highlight a few that are unrelated to each other." And then, written at the bottom of the page, "Kate, University of California at Berkeley? Please come see me during lunch period." What does that mean? And, I hate one on ones with her. She's so intimidating!

I walk into the empty classroom with as much confidence as I can muster. Mrs. Harrington looks up so I walk towards her while simultaneously, rummaging for my admissions essay in my backpack. She interrupts my efforts by saying, "I don't need to see your paper. Sit down; I want to discuss your choice of university."

"Oh, okay," I mutter.

"I understand that Cal is your first choice? Do you have others?"

"I really want to attend Cal. But, yeah, I will apply to others as back -ups. Isn't that what you said to do?"

"Yes, I recommend a diverse application approach but in your case, you may have to rely on those back -ups." My heart sinks as she continues. "The counselors provided me with the Pre-SAT scores of the students in my Honors Class. I matched them up against their university of choice. While you have stellar grades and wonderful extra-curricular, your SAT scores will need to be much higher than your Pre-SAT. Of all the UC schools, Cal and UCLA have the most rigorous admissions. . Your application will need to be nearly perfect. I suggest you take a SAT class to prepare yourself for the test."

Stunned I say, "Okay, I'll look into it."

As an add-on she says, "I don't mean to be harsh but I have to help you be realistic."

"Okay, thanks." Why in the world did I thank her? And, by the way, 'harsh' might be an understatement.

I slink out with my head markedly lower than when I arrived ten minutes earlier.

I eat lunch from the vending machines instead of finding the group in the cafeteria. How dare she cast doubt? What a buzz-kill that woman is.

❧ ❧ ❧

I'm still simmering about the meeting with Mrs. Harrington. Now I'm a bundle of nerves over the SAT's thanks to her! I march into the house and find my mom right away. "Mom, you are never going to believe what my English teacher said to me today!"

My mom's head spins around quickly. "What. What did she say?"

I share the encounter with her. I finish the story and catch mom's reaction. She pauses a little too long and then her eyes squint to suggest some quick thinking is occurring on her part. I figure she feels like she needs to get this response right to keep my wavering confidence intact.

"Well," she starts slowly, "surely she underestimates you. What do you think would be helpful to prepare so you go into the test confident?"

"I don't know," I reply exasperated. "I wish she wouldn't have said anything. I was going to study hard anyway. Now I don't think that is enough. Maybe I need a SAT class or tutor or something?"

"Okay, we'll find out what will work with your schedule. I'll ask around to find out what our options are. Sound good?"

"Yeah, that's good. Thanks."

"Do you want me to have a discussion with Mrs. Harrington about how this affected you? She should know."

"No way! Definitely not. It would only make it worse." I am certain of that. Mrs. Harrington doesn't like any signs of weakness.

From that day forward, SAT Saturday was deemed, "Black SAT". I've never been so uncomfortable. SAT testing is this weekend. And, the amount of studying I am doing is completely negated by the thoughts of doubt that continue to haunt me.

I try to shake it by studying more but it only makes it worse. It's like each hour of studying fertilizes a big, monster plant of self doubt. Instead of resisting this ominous feeling, I need to be nurturing my self confidence! Of course, the clover tree! It's time to invoke the clover tree as a last ditch effort. Why didn't I think of it sooner?

Chapter Twenty Two

By the time my dad comes home from work, I'm still in a tizzy. He already received the news via mom, Kelsey or whoever heard my ranting through our suburban walls. He was calm. He had to be. No one else in the family was capable of it. I was freaking out at the prospect of not getting what I want.

I'm sure he wanted to walk in and curse, rant and possibly hit a pillow or two on my behalf; but, no, he puts down his briefcase and takes me aside. I crumble. Mom and Kelsey had given me their support, but this was the final voice. And that voice said, "I'm sorry."

My blood was boiling but I felt weaker than ever. "Dad, I am so mad! I worked so hard! I went to that stupid SAT class, I studied hard, I visualized the test but these scores will never get me into Cal! I did everything I could and the clover tree let me down."

Dad replied, "Who let you down?"

"The clover tree," I replied.

"*Hmmm.* You know the clover tree cannot let you down. It's universally true and honest in its offerings. What happened?"

"I DON'T KNOW!" I shout in my fury.

"What are the rules of the clover tree?" my dad presses.

I am so annoyed at this line of questioning on my darkest day;

I could strangle him. Yet, I fall apart even further and surprising myself that I'm unraveling so much.

Dad couldn't stand the despair I'm displaying. He hugs me hard and says, "Honey, the universe takes its cues from you. When did you stop believing in yourself?"

And I knew.

There is no toast at dinner; nothing to celebrate today after the terrible SAT news. I retreat to my room to listen to music. I don't even want to finish my homework. What does a good GPA matter now? I'm not gonna get into Cal. I look up at the clover labeled, GOOD SAT SCORE and consider what happened. I know that Mrs. Harrington planted a lot of doubt in me. She shook my confidence. But, I thought I took control by studying hard and becoming prepared. I hear dad enter his office. I want to talk it out.

"You have a sec?" I melt into the spare chair across from his desk assuming he will stop everything and talk to me.

Of course, he will. "Yep, what's up?"

"Can we revisit the SAT thing?"

"Sure."

"You asked me when I stopped believing and I get that. My confidence was really shattered after my conversation with Mrs. Harrington. But, doesn't the clover tree give me the power to overcome it, just by asking for a different outcome? What I mean is, I labeled a clover GOOD SAT SCORE and did the visualization and I studied really hard. Why wasn't that enough?"

"You must not have truly believed in your ability. Like I said, the clovers, when invoked properly, are not capable of disappointing you. In this case you asked a lot of the clover, given where you started. What did you call SAT day?"

"Black Saturday; I think it's clever, and appropriate."

"That's not making me think that you changed your thoughts about the test," he states.

"I hate that test. It doesn't necessarily gauge intelligence. It gauges how well you can take a standardized test. It's totally unfair," I insist.

"There are a lot of people and universities that agree with you; however, it is part of the system. First of all, do not spend time studying for that test one more minute. You are well prepared." I like this advice already. He continues, "I suggest you change your thoughts that surround the test."

"What does that mean?"

"It means, carry a different thought pattern than, 'It's stupid, unfair, etc'. I think this is the piece that is missing. If you can perceive the test as meaningful and easy and believe how prepared you are, you could have a different outcome."

"No more studying? I just have to LOVE the SAT?" I say sarcastically.

"Pretty much; but, really believe it. Make it true for you."

"Alright-y, I'll give it a go. There's another chance to take it coming up soon. I have nothing to lose and everything to gain!"

"That's a good attitude."

"If a good attitude gets me into Cal then I am the most positive gal on the planet!"

"Cal or no Cal, a good attitude has its own rewards."

"Alright, alright; I get it. Good night."

With her left hand, mom pushes a freshly blended smoothie across the table. With her right hand, she pushes an envelope across the table toward me. I'm puzzled.

"Looks like SAT scores," mom suggests. I get a pit in my stomach. I had managed to put them out of my mind. Guess it's time for me to answer to the standardized test gods. I pull the envelope off the table and gingerly open it.

Mom remembers the last time SAT scores arrived. "Whatever the results, it will be okay."

"I know." I pull out the single sheet of paper. I quickly peruse my fate.

Mom is searching my face for clues. There are probably many. I sigh, "Better."

"Great!" mom chimes in.

"But not good enough for Cal, I'm sure."

"Let me see," she says. I hand her the results.

"You never know. With all your other stuff, you could get in," she reminds me.

"I'll need a compassionate admissions officer."

"Maybe not; these are good scores Kate. Don't beat yourself up about it."

I hear her say, "Good scores". They are good scores, but not great.

"I'll be right back Mom." I jump out of my chair and run back to my room. Looking up at my clover tree I find what I am looking for, the SAT clover. In all its glory, it is labeled, GOOD SAT SCORES. Good! What was I thinking? I need GREAT SAT scores for Cal. If the clover could talk it would remind me that it delivered what I asked for. It's a cruel joke and I'm not laughing. Dad might though.

He didn't laugh but his eyes crinkled in amusement. Even the devoted owner of the clover field is in awe of its power. And accuracy!

"That is incredible validation of what you manifested for yourself. That aside, I know you are disappointed. How are you doing?" dad asks with a look of slight concern on his face.

"Okay, I guess. I'm not used to my hard work not paying off. It doesn't feel good."

"It paid off, honey. You just have very high expectations. You will have a lot of choices for college; not to worry."

"It's just hard changing my plan. It seemed so foolproof."

"There are no guarantees. Even with a good plan. Look at

my work. I hire architects to draft blueprints so we have a clear plan when we start to build. But, does it ever go smoothly? Never! Just like a construction project, your life will not always go smoothly. But, you can control its outcome through your attitude and thoughts that surround the plan you have for yourself."

"It's hard for me to change my thoughts."

"Thoughts are powerful but not tangible. I know I've talked to you about 'changing' your thoughts but I should have phrased it differently. You can't really 'change' your thoughts. But you can replace them with new ones that serve you better."

"Like getting a new pair of jeans when my old ones get too small?"

Dad laughs, "Kinda."

CHAPTER TWENTY THREE

I am lying on the floor listening to music, visualizing the State High School Championship game. I have high hopes for myself and the team. While I have entertained the idea of great success every year, this year's confidence is realistic. Under the evolving leadership from Coach Kelly, the girls' soccer program at BHS has improved dramatically. That first year together was bumpy. But, the greatness we hoped for back then is the success we've earned now. So, I'm invoking my ritual of visualization to prepare for tomorrow's game. It helps my nerves and gives me confidence. With the music as a backdrop, I am crafting pass after pass to my forward line. They are lining the net with goals to secure victory. I don't hear my dad enter my room but I sense him so I snap out of it.

"Hey Dad."

"Hi honey. I just wanted to tell you 'Good luck tomorrow'. You all have worked hard for this opportunity."

My mom is walking by and pokes her head in offering, "Remember to have fun too!"

"I know mom! Soccer is my favorite thing in the whole world. I always have fun!"

"Well good. Then why don't you score a few goals and ensure that we all have fun watching you win!" She snickers and continues down the hallway.

Dad smiles and adds, "Well, it's true. Mom and I sure have enjoyed this soccer experience. And, it is fun to cheer on a big win. It has been great watching you represent BHS so well."

"I was just thinking about how much we've improved over the last three years. We were like, 2-6 my freshman year!"

"And now, you are vying for the State title. It is a huge accomplishment for you girls. How is Coach Kelly holding up?" dad asks. He's always liked Coach Kelly.

"I've never felt so much nervous tension from her before. She goes from excited and goofy to snappy, 'Ladies! Focus! We have to get this set play down! This could be an easy goal given the chance.' Luckily we know she's all jazzed up so we just let her go. She even got a sub for herself yesterday so she could spend time researching our opponent."

"That's serious business," he smiles, "She's invested a lot of time and patience. This is her reward."

"She's improved right along with us, huh?" It's a question and an observation.

"You were an eclectic bunch of players when she arrived. Now you are a team."

"True. We all have the common denominator that we want to win for our school. It's not like we are competing so much for playing time or a chance at the National Team; it feels really 'normal.' "

"That's an interesting choice of words. Your take on soccer is hardly 'normal.' But, I like the new perspective! Love you honey."

The energy in the locker room is off the charts! Our JV team, spearheaded by the starting center back, Kelsey Malone, decorated our lockers with posters of encouragement and we can hear the band warming up outside. It is crisp and cold so Coach Kelly instructs us to put on our Under Armour since it is a night game;

and it's under the lights—which is extra exciting! The stands will be full of our friends and families. We trickle onto the field to warm up. Before Coach corrals us, my family approaches. They are all so supportive and brimming with excitement. My dad can barely contain himself, "Next year I will be watching both Malone girls on this soccer pitch!" Wearing her JV Soccer hoodie, Kelsey smiles eagerly knowing that a spot on Varsity is a likely prospect next year. Mom does not want to look ahead, "Joe, let's stay in the present, please. First things, first! Kate, play well sweetie!" Kelsey gives me a hug and dad, a customary squeeze to my shoulders and winks; his gesture of approval and confidence. We break up and then mom says, "A photo, we need a family photo under the lights!"

The text from Morgan came through immediately after the game, "THAT SUCKS. C U OUTSIDE THE LOCKER ROOM." I'm taking the loss hard. I'm replaying the game over and over in my head while I'm showering up. It's futile. I can't change the outcome. One fluke goal from the other team and the Championship was determined. Soccer is brutal that way. Coach Kelly could barely muster a speech as her disappointment equaled ours. She didn't say much about the game since we played well. It was just a last minute misstep that started with the forward line and continued through each line of defense until the shot ricocheted off our sweeper into the goal. It wasn't really her fault although I wanted to her to shoulder all the blame so I could unburden myself. But instead, with the help of Coach's locker room speech, I realized it was a complete team meltdown in the last two minutes. I felt bad for the seniors; after all, I had another chance to bring the Championship to BHS. Outside the locker room Morgan was the first to console me.

"I'm sorry Kate. You played great though."

"Thanks Morgan. We'll do it next year."

"Yeah, you will." She's always so positive.

Before we could continue, my family hedged on in.

"Oh, sweetie." The way my mom says it makes me feel worse. I feel like I let them down.

"Hi Mom." I'm annoyed.

Dad comes up next and says, "Great effort out there, Kate." I know he means it, but I also know how passionate he is about winning; the feeling that I let them down returns. Geez.

Kelsey approaches and gives me a hip check. "Next year you'll have me out there to help you out. We'll win the trophy together." The levity is perfect.

"Yep, Kelse, you are right; divine timing. We need to do it together!"

I feel better... for now.

But in the end, everyone is bummed. First, a glorious season and then the grand finale had to end in a chump loss. To make matters worse, I am named to the 3A All State SECOND team, not the first; where several of my teammates are placed. My reaction to the news is not one of my finer moments. A mild tantrum in front of my teammates is not what a Team Captain should model. Later, as I lay in my room ashamed, my dad walks in. I expect him to reprimand me but instead he says, "I didn't know you were so hard on yourself." His compassion and the truth of his words overtake me. I burst out crying. In my world, this is one of the worst days of my life.

"But Dad, I worked so hard! We should have won that game. And, I should be on the FIRST All State 3A team! I'm a better player than some of those girls!"

"I don't disagree with you Kate, but who knows what was factored in. You should be very proud of yourself and your leadership in getting your team to the High School Championship. It hurts me too, that you didn't receive the recognition you deserve, but it is more upsetting to me that you can't cut yourself some slack."

"Dad, it's just a nightmare. I am Team Captain. We lost. I didn't get chosen. Soccer is everything to me. I feel like I failed myself. How am I going to attend the awards ceremony and watch Sara get up and accept the First Team honors when I should be there!?"

He let me vent some more. The more I talked, the less I made sense. My ego was out of control on this one and I could tell my dad was trying to process it all.

"Kate, do you hear what you are saying? What I am hearing from you is that you led your team to the 3A Championship but you LOST. You excelled as a player all year; yet, you were named to the Second 3A team, not the first. The standards you set for yourself are extremely high." He continues, "When you fall short of these lofty expectations, you are profoundly disappointed in yourself. Linking your self worth to perfection is a flawed formula. Feeling success and worthiness should not be contingent on all of these external factors."

In general, I was perfectly content striving for perfection. Up until now, it had mostly worked out for me. Sure, I was taking these soccer setbacks hard, but I didn't think it was affecting my confidence at all.

"But Dad, I do believe in myself. I am confident."

"Why are you confident?" he asks.

I proceed to rattle off my list of accomplishments.

"Yes, those are certainly reasons to feel confident. Your mom and I are very proud of you and all you have accomplished. But tell me, do you need that resume of accomplishments to love yourself?"

"What?"

"Is your list of accomplishments directly linked to how you feel about yourself?"

I consider the mammoth question he just posed and reply, "Yep."

"Honey that is all I want you to think about on this journey of life. Can you find internal reasons to love yourself as well? Because, if your impressive list went away, what would you see in the mirror? If you could no longer say, 'that is Kate—the awesome soccer player, good friend, Math whiz' could you still feel self worth? Is it possible for your confidence and joy to come from a feeling of general self-acceptance? Would it be okay to be flawed?"

"Flawed? "

"Yes, flawed. Or, as your mom would say, 'warts and all'."

I briefly ponder his question. And dad spends the wait time smoothing out his eyebrows in anticipation. I go with my first reaction anyway, "No. Flaws are not acceptable."

As if the lag time (or eyebrow maintenance) provided more ideas on the subject, he picks up where he left off. "This is not to say that I want you to stop setting goals and striving for success because you have a lot of gifts to offer this world. But your gifts will shine even brighter if you could be less demanding of yourself. Try it out. You are such a kind daughter, sister and friend. See what it feels like to be as kind and forgiving to yourself as you are to everyone else."

Now that kind of makes some sense. Kindness, forgiveness; my formula of perfection does not allow for me to be very kind or forgiving of myself. While all of this was sinking in, I do have one obvious truth to point out.

"Well Dad, I will take this under consideration since it seems to me that the old dude offering this sage advice comes from a long history of perfectionist behavior himself."

With a smile he says, "Touché," and gives me a light, playful punch to the arm. "I'm just trying to save you the 40 years it took me to figure it out."

With another smile, he leaves my room but my mind keeps churning over what he said. I'm about to turn on some music but instead I decide to revisit something that has worked so well before. I pulled out my clover tree and labeled the clover closest to the top. Presiding over all the other clovers was my newest creation, SELF LOVE. My heart answered with a very strong thought, "Be in awe of your being-ness—just BE".

CHAPTER TWENTY FOUR

I can barely keep my eyes open driving home from soccer practice. School soccer ended and the Premier Coaches could hardly wait to get us back. Coach Tom is working us hard, running lines, intense drills all the while reminding us of our upcoming season and State Cup tournament in just a few months. Luckily, Sara is in the car and clearly isn't as exhausted as I am since she is producing nonstop chatter. She always has a story to tell. Tonight I'm not bothered; it keeps me alert.

I drop her off in the neighborhood and head home. I still have homework and I desperately need a shower and dinner. It might be another long night. I turn the corner onto my street and notice my driveway full of cars. Dang! My mom didn't warn me about hosting Book Club tonight. I'm so annoyed. This means I'll have to be cordial to all the lady friends before I can retreat to my room. Definitely a long night ahead!

I park on the street since I can't get into the garage. I'll have to remember to ask my dad to move the car inside later. I grab my soccer pack and lumber up the walkway. As I put my hand on the mudroom door, my stomach unexpectedly lurches in dread. "What a strange reaction," I think to myself. I enter the house without announcing myself since they are already expecting me; plus I don't want to interrupt the lively book discussion.

The next series of events surprises everyone. No one hears

me come in so when I turn the corner the adults huddled around the kitchen island are startled and my heart misses a beat upon realizing that there is no book club meeting. Suddenly I realize that my feeling of dread might have some merit.

I didn't see my mom amongst the adults in the kitchen but my mom, slumped in the corner of the couch sees me. It seems like slow motion. I can tell she is rushing but her body looks so heavy that it can't gain momentum to reach me quickly. Her face is swollen from crying yet not red and flush but ashen. In the time it takes her to travel to me I glance around the kitchen to see my uncles, our best friends and neighbors all with looks of pity and despair. The dread in my stomach moves toward my throat and I want to throw up as I anticipate the news.

"Kate," my mom wails, "there has been a terrible accident. Your dad, his car, a semi truck, the tire flew off. Oh my God, your father is dead."

She tries to hug me but I reel back, crumbling to the ground in disbelief and shock; the floor bracing me for the impending agony. And then, for whatever reason, I cover my eyes. I don't cover my mouth to stifle my cries; but, instead, pull my hands to my face and yearn to be invisible, no longer here, experiencing this reality. Then, as quickly as I fell to the ground, I am up pacing throughout the house crazed, "NO, NO, NO!" I punch pillows and kick furniture. I can't believe just an hour ago I was playing soccer, liberated and untouched by tragedy. How did I not feel my dad leaving me? Am I so self absorbed that when he left I could still carry on like nothing was different? I expected that I would just "know" but I didn't. I am totally blindsided by this event and I become robot-like as the pain is unbearable. I'm inconsolable and I repel any form of physical touch as it made me more present and human. I think: will I ever stop crying? I heave in despair. Who knew that crying could be so physical? But it wasn't just crying… it was grief. It's in those first moments of grief when it takes on a life of its own and you pray it is a dream.

The news traveled fast; literally. The accident was all over the evening newscast although they didn't reveal the name of the deceased. An aberrant blown tire off a semi flew into the windshield of my dad's car. The news suggested that dad probably died from the impact of the tire but the car went 360 degrees over the median into oncoming traffic and then down a ravine. I'm pretty sure his spirit was long gone before he hit the ravine. Nevertheless, by the time our community heard of the tragedy on the news, they were already quite familiar with the story.

CHAPTER TWENTY FIVE

Mom looks so sad and sallow walking down the stairs from their bedroom. We are going to the mortuary for final arrangements. It's all so surreal. So much so that I can actually convince myself it didn't happen. I look at the door toward the garage and I can trick my mind for an instant that he might walk right through the door. It offers a few seconds of respite but all too soon, the agony sets back in. It doesn't appear as though my mom has any technique for a mental or emotional break. She has already lost a ton of weight and the sadness distorts her face.

It is awful panning our faces desperately looking for any of the former sparkle. The pain is hard enough to endure myself, but I am forced to look at my heartbroken reflection in the faces of my mom and sister, which makes it even worse.

We gather up our purses, papers and sadness as we move toward the garage. Mom hands me the keys, "You okay to drive?"

"Yeah Mom, I can drive."

"Thanks sweetie. I'm tired."

"I understand."

Church or no church for the memorial service is the pressing question. We have been littered with questions since dad died and the three of us are walking around like zombies. I'm quite certain Mom will never remember these days. She looks like a ghost and for the first time in our lives, she can't comfort us. Thanks to our neighbor, Mrs. Potter, there is never a dull moment. And sure enough, she comes bounding in, intercepting us. "Sacred Heart is available for Joe's service. I can make all the arrangements," she insists.

Mom squeaks out an answer, "I'm not sure. We haven't attended church in years." I think, "Years? I'm 17 and can't remember ever attending regularly."

"Once a parishioner, always a parishioner Alyson; rest assured. You will need a space that large anyway. It will be packed. We'll go over and meet Father Curran later."

"I'm not concerned about the space or logistics. I need to consider what Joe would want."

"Didn't he grow up attending church?" asks Mrs. Potter.

"Yes. He did all of it as a child. And, he did insist the girls were baptized Catholic. That's when we attended church regularly."

"Why did you stop attending?"

"Oh, the kids were growing up and we kind of lost interest, I guess."

"So, you didn't have a 'falling out' with the church?" she politely asks.

"No, no not at all; Joe had a philosophy about life and faith that somehow made sitting in a church pew irrelevant." I can tell that mom's explanation makes no sense to Mrs. Potter. But, I had been at the receiving end of many of dad's "teachings" so I know exactly what she means. Mrs. Potter glosses over mom's comment. I get the sense she's going to push this one through.

"Why don't you come meet Father Curran and maybe that will help you decide," she offers.

"Okay. Should the girls come?"

"If they want to, sure." Mrs. Potter probably doesn't understand why we would go when she has everything under control.

"Girls you should come." It's really not a request.

"Okay," with a heavy sigh, I agree. Nothing is negotiable right now. A second sigh escapes me but mom doesn't notice that one either. In my former life she would have said, "Oh, sweetie. What's wrong?" Instead, adult responsibilities consume my newly defined adolescence and life as I knew it with friends and soccer is slipping away.

"Okay," says Kelsey, following my lead.

My friend's pleas to take me out will go unanswered another day.

I remember the church from the random times we attended over the years. It's not ornate at all. But the priest is. Father Curran is robust, like an Irish Santa Claus. His priestly robe is generously draped over him. All he needs is a thick black patent leather belt cinched around his belly to complete the look. Dad would really like him. When he greets us his outstretched hand sports a large ring with a hefty red stone mimicking the Super Bowl rings football players show off during their SportsCenter interviews. When he grasps my hand, I can feel his compassion course through my body. He repeats the action with each of us and then we collectively sit down. He has a ton of questions for us about dad and then mom pulls out a few photos.

"He has such friendly, lively eyes," Father Curran points out.

"Yes, Joe's eyes were very blue and very expressive," Mom trails off. I hate hearing his name in past tense.

Father Curran outlines what the service might include. Mom politely interrupts him, "Will it be a full mass?"

"Yes, usually it is. Even though your husband hadn't attended church recently, he has a long history of being a devoted Catholic. And, from what I understand, many of his friends are members of our congregation. With such a large Catholic presence at his funeral, I do think a full mass is appropriate."

"Including Communion?" she asks.

"Mass is the means through which we express the Eucharist.

Are you talking about the 'Rite of Communion' where we offer bread and wine?" Father asks.

As I sit here I realize I know very little about church. Mom might be thinking the same thing.

"Yes. I guess I am," my mom answers. "When everyone else gets up to join the procession for Communion I will feel like an outsider. I don't want to feel like I don't belong at my husband's funeral."

"I understand. It's a sign of unity within our faith to take Communion. A confirmed Catholic takes Communion with the understanding that Christ is present. It's really about the belief system attached to the ritual more than eating bread and drinking a sip of wine." My ears perk up. Somehow this is making sense. "You see, we believe that the consecrated bread and wine is more than a symbol; the essence of Christ is within us."

I think about how weird that must feel.

He continues, "That being said, it is a pastoral decision and in my opinion it goes against the idea of Communion to deny it. So you should feel free to join the rest of the parish."

"That's very compassionate Father Curran. However, I'm not sure I feel comfortable with it anyway. What about the girls?"

"So, the girls are baptized Catholic?"

"Yes, both of them were baptized here, actually," mom confirms.

"It's up to them, but they could take communion at the service," Father replies. It seems like special treatment. Then he adds, "I would encourage them to consider developing their faith."

I jump in, "I wouldn't know what to do during the taking of Communion part."

"I could take you through the ritual, but I will insist you let me explain how the ritual and the belief must go hand in hand," Father offers.

Mom says, "Thanks for your sensitivity to our needs and unusual situation. We will discuss it first."

I am going to talk to Kelsey but I'm personally not going to leave mom stranded while I take communion. As far as I'm concerned, all the practicing Catholics can commune on dad's behalf.

Father Curran moves on by suggesting readings and songs. He asks, "Do you have anything special you want to include?" Mom suggests a song by Enya which won't be found in the hymnal book, by the way. Father Curran is really accommodating. There are a few more questions about readers, pallbearers and flowers. Dad's unexpected death makes these details all the more excruciating. What would *he* want? We follow our hearts with the decisions and know that as for the rest of the details, Mrs. Potter will take care of them or delegate. However, mom insists on arranging for the flowers. I decide I want the mass program pamphlet to be special. I ask Morgan's mom to help me. She accepts the daunting task of memorializing my dad for me.

I find Kelsey in her room with a mountain of art supplies on her bed.

"Where'd you get all this stuff?"

"I always ask for art and craft supplies for my birthday. They just added up."

"What are you doing with it?"

"I'm going to start using it. The counselor at school thought art might help me deal with dad dying."

"You've been talking to a counselor?"

"Yeah, I broke down crying in Math one day and my teacher sent me to the office to 're-group.' Not very sensitive, I must say; but anyway, I went and my counselor was really nice. I didn't even know you could really go talk to one."

"Kelsey, why didn't you tell me?"

"Oh, Kate, you are like mom's right-hand at the moment; being the oldest and stuff. I couldn't burden you with *me*."

"Omigosh. Kelse, I want you to lean on me. I want to lean on you! Yeah, I'm overwhelmed but I always want to help you." The familiar tears fill our eyes and I move in next to her.

"Thanks Kate." She says choking back heavy sobs that want to erupt.

"It's a lot. I hope we can get through this. Anyway, the art thing sounds like a good idea," I say as I wonder what might help me endure this journey.

"So, why'd you come in here in the first place?" I can tell she wants to get back to organizing her supplies.

"Oh yeah, I came in to talk to you about the funeral." I change gears into operational mode. "What do you think about Father Curran?"

"I like him a lot. He's so friendly." Like Santa Claus, I consider the likeness again.

"Yeah, I think he'll do a good job." Although I am curious how the church explains untimely death. "What do you think about doing the Communion thing?"

"I don't care. I feel like dad would want us to do it but since mom can't...," she trails off.

"I would hate to leave mom stranded in the pew," I say.

"Me too," she emphatically agrees.

"You know what else?" I have one more point even though that's probably a good enough reason.

"What?" Kelsey asks.

"When Father Curran explained how the ritual and the belief needed to go together, I was thinking about our clover trees and how it wouldn't work for us if we didn't have our unfaltering belief in it. And that maybe we shouldn't take communion since we haven't done the work to understand the belief system behind it."

"That's a lot of thinking, Kate. I just thought it might be interesting to try something new."

"Well, our Catholic friends can represent us. We should stick together."

"Sounds good," Kelsey agrees as she pulls out some paints. "I'll let mom know," I say as I exit her room.

All eyes are on the Malone girls as we enter the church. The sadness is palpable. Morgan hands me a program on my way in. It looks awesome. Dad is smiling right at me. Although, really, I'm sure he is doing more than that because I'm not sure how mom is putting one foot in front of the other right now. She must have some divine help. We sit in the front and I think how I would rather be in the front row of something other than my dad's funeral.

Madi's family is nearby and her mom has a pile of used Kleenex on her lap already. I know that all eyes are on us but I want to look around. I turn my head and rotate it fast enough so I don't lock eyes with anyone. The church is packed. There are even people standing in the back. I hope dad realized while he was alive how many people liked him.

Father Curran looks more like a priest today than Santa Claus. His robes are elegant and his demeanor is less jolly than the other day. Kelsey is on the right side of mom; I'm on the left. Mom is very stoic today. Father Curran greets the congregation and begins, "It is not God's will to take a young father from his family." Where's he going with this? I thought the church had more answers than just wiggling off the hook. "It was an accident that took Joe Malone from this earth, not God." He speaks of the grace of God and dad's immortality because of his faith, but I'm processing only bits and pieces. Despite his faith and good intentions, Father Curran's explanation isn't all that comforting to me. I'm thinking I want to have my funeral outside in a big soccer stadium. I feel claustrophobic in here.

However, I glance over at Kelsey and she is mesmerized. In fact, she looks peaceful. The church filled with people must make her feel safe. And, I'm glad his words make sense to her. Maybe

I should be more attentive. Nevertheless, I choose to look at the program instead of listening.

The program is an everlasting tribute; the equivalent of a funeral "party favor". It is something by which our guests, my dad's friends and family can keep to remember him. The photo on the front is perfect. Mom found it. In the original photo, she is standing right next to him. She is cropped out for purposes of highlighting my dad, his signature smile and expressive eyes. But, it makes more sense that she is next to him because his eyes reflect love and joy. It's bittersweet to look at this one-dimensional photo of the father who was taken too early. I flip the program over and stare at the Malone Family Christmas photo. We took it over the summer in the backyard before the heat wreaked havoc on mom's garden. It occurs to me that it never made it onto a Christmas card. Right below the photo is dad's favorite toast: "The Irish are at their best when there is something to celebrate!" And it goes on to say, "Following the service, please join us at the Bellevue Athletic Club to **celebrate** the life of a wonderful husband, father, brother and friend. With love: Alyson, Katherine and Kelsey Malone." I should have stopped reading because I was still holding myself together.

On the inside, the memorial program outlines the whole service. With it being a full mass, the entire right side of the program is packed. On the left, she included a poem that was not part of the stuff I gave her:

> "When I come to the end of the road /And the sun has set for me,
> I want no rites in a gloom-filled room. /Why cry for a soul set free.
> Miss me a little…but not too long /And not with your head bowed low.
> Remember the love that we once shared. /Miss me… but let me go.
> For this is a journey we all must take /And each must go alone.

It's all part of the Master's plan, /A step on the road to home.
When you are lonely and sick of heart, /Go to the friends we know
And bury your sorrows in doing good deeds. /Miss me…but let me go."
Author Unknown

Tears are on their way as I realize that the poem marries my dad's religious background and spiritual journey perfectly. "I want no rites in a gloom-filled room. /Why cry for a soul set free…. For this is a journey we all must take/And each must go alone. It's all part of the Master's plan, /A step on the road to home." In his death, he still finds the right words to say.

As if Father Curran knows I'm not paying attention, he leaves the podium and walks toward us. As the hundreds of friends watch on, he kneels before us and touches each of our foreheads individually with a blessing. Then, for all to hear, he reminds us how much my dad "Loved his girls". Mom breaks down sobbing. Morgan's mom, sitting directly behind her touches her shoulder. Kelsey and I lean up against her as if to keep her from toppling over. Father Curran's parting comments to us are, "You will make him proud and you will be fine." He emphasizes "will". Right now, I don't believe him.

Trailing the casket out of the church I see Ryan leaning against a back wall. His face is contorted when our eyes lock. It's possible he's thinking the same thing I am, "Sadness isn't a good look."

CHAPTER TWENTY SIX

You really need silence to grieve. With our friends and family hovering with concern and food, the three of us have been able to stave off reality. And then, like the flick of a light switch, the hovering and meal delivery stopped. Mrs. Potter's cinnamon rolls no longer appear on our front porch and our mainstay casseroles have dwindled from our freezer and fridge. I get it. Life goes on. For others, the trivialities of life still consume their daily existence. For us, life is much different. And as the reality that we are on our own seeps in, I'm daunted by buoying this amount of grief on my own. It's time for the Malone girls to start healing. For me, the logical outlet is to get back to the soccer pitch and reconnect with my friends.

I enjoy a wonderful reception from my teammates as they bombard me in a big group hug. I'm hopeful this will be a great place to recover.

In general, soccer practice proves to be a decent distraction. Yet, my mind wanders thinking of my dad and how much he loved watching me play and interacting with my teammates. Fortunately, the drills move quickly so I don't stay lost too long. There's always a chance I will well up in tears when I start remembering my dad and I hate when I cry in public because it makes everyone uncomfortable. While my soccer family brings me comfort, they too have chosen silence on the topic of my dad's death. Maybe they think it helps but it doesn't. I really need people to acknowledge IT. The weight of the grief is eating at me from the inside out. I'm pretty sure I can't shoulder this alone.

"Kate!" Coach yells. "Mark your player."

My momentary lapse ends and I am back pretending that everything is okay.

Right now as I sit at the lunch table, the conversation seems so trivial. The new store in the mall is a hot topic and Devyn's new car is getting a lot of play too. I wonder if they know how they sound. Or, are they just jabbering about nonsense to fill up the void that might become, "Kate's Dad Died"? I know that in my former life, I didn't really think that talking about the mall was nonsense, so they probably don't either. In fact, even though my lens on life is different and currently, quite grey, I do hope that I can get back to the place where discussing skinny leg or boot cut jeans is relatively important again. Just as I'm trying to find meaning in their conversation, Devyn snaps me out of my wandering.

"Kate, you have been so aloof. What is wrong with you? It feels like you are jealous of me and my new car."

"What?" The stinger comment definitely snaps me back to reality.

"Yeah, you just seem so disinterested in what we are all doing; like you are jealous, or maybe even better than us."

I am so stunned, I can barely react. These are my friends. Is it so hard to understand that I am trying to be happy for them, but I cannot find an ounce of happiness for myself? I muster up some words and courage and send a stinger right back,

"No Devyn, I'm not jealous of your car. I'm happy for you. What I am jealous about is that you all have fathers that are alive!" I grab the rest of my lunch, toss it in the trash and walk out of the lunchroom.

What's it going to take to find joy and direction again in my rudderless life?

As I approach the house, I notice our front door is painted blue. It used to be black but now it's blue. It's also open. "Mom! Why is our door blue?"

"Hi sweetie; Mr. Harris came by today with this idea."

"To paint the door?" I ask with a look of confusion on my face.

"Well, you know he is one of dad's Irish buddies. Part of the St. Patrick's day card list."

"Oh, yeah. Mr. 'Mc-Harris'. But, what does that have to do with changing the color of our front door?"

"Well, after he promised to keep the St. Patrick's Day card tradition going in honor of dad he shared an Irish proverb about painting a door in hard times. Here, I have the note he wrote. The proverb goes like this: *Paint a door when times are rough.* " It sounds like there should be more to it, but that's all that is written in the card. He could have made it up for all we know.

"And you let him paint our door because of that?" I'm incredulous. Mom normally doesn't change things so easily.

"He was so excited about it and I could just tell he felt helpless. This seemed like a way for him to do something positive."

"And now we have a blue door," I point out.

"I know it's crazy. But after he finished and I saw how happy he was, it seemed worth it. And, then I came inside and I started laughing at the absurdity of it all and realized it was the first time I have laughed since the accident."

"That's really good," I admit.

"And there's a part of me that feels like dad had a hand in it." I can tell it brings her comfort to say this.

"I wouldn't be surprised. It sounds like something he would do." I imagine dad up in heaven slapping his leg, his blue eyes crinkled in delight.

"I agree. How was school today?"

"Terrible. Like every day."

"What happened?"

"No one understands."

"It's a tough club to join. Especially at your age, and no one else has been through it."

"And I don't want them to. But today, I was really trying not to be 'the girl whose dad died' and Devyn misinterpreted my silence as being jealous."

"Oh, that name again," my mom sighs.

"It was her today, but other days it's someone else saying something stupid. And, practically the whole school is walking on eggshells with looks of pity when I'm around."

"Sweetie, your schoolmates really don't know what to do. I'm having the same problem. None of my friends have lost their husbands, many not even their fathers. I spent some time being mad at the insensitivity or stupidity too. When I realized that their intentions were to comfort me, it helped. At this point, I'm grateful for the people that actually acknowledge it," mom admits. "Wouldn't it be even worse if they ignored you entirely, don't you think? Then you would be alone."

"I guess."

"At least Devyn is treating you the same as always."

"No doubt!" I say as we laugh together about it. It feels good to laugh together again.

CHAPTER TWENTY SEVEN

I am home alone tonight. Morgan's mom coaxed my mom into joining her at the movies. Kelsey's at a friend's for dinner. There is a frozen casserole on the counter with instructions but I'm not hungry. My mind is wandering as I lie on my bed. I'm not sure I enjoy being alone with my thoughts these days. I miss my dad so much and the quiet house compounds the loss. I roll over to grab my IPod, so as to break the silence. As I lean over to grab it, I glance up at my clover tree. One of my last additions stares back at me, SELF LOVE. I remember that day just a few months ago, dad came into my room after the State Championship loss. Omigosh; a wave of panic sets in because I can't remember what he said! I try to playback the conversation but my mind draws a blank! Slowly, snippets start to return, "What do you see in the mirror?"; "Be kind to yourself". But, my racing mind is obstructing the memories from coming back to life. I take a deep breath which helps temporarily, and then I am pounding my pillow in frustration! Oh, how I took for granted his accessible guidance and wisdom while he was here. Now I am relying on fleeting scraps of advice that I still don't entirely understand. "Dad," I yell, "what did you mean by finding my confidence from internal sources?" And, then in a mix of anger and sadness I ask, "Daddy, why did you leave me? I have more to learn from you!" I am crying, crying, crying. It exhausts me so much, I fall asleep.

My sister's path through grief is church. Mom and I support her, of course. She is finding her way, as we are finding ours. Sitting in a church pew certainly isn't going to make things worse for her, and mom and I understand that. She marches off with the neighbors to church and we are thankful for their generosity. Actually, it's not that mom and I even discuss all of this, the three of us are in three separate worlds; yet, we have this knowing, this understanding that we are each doing our best to endure the reality that faces us.

This evening, Kelsey came home and knocked on my bedroom door. I was working on homework, it was deadly silent and I was grateful for the interruption. Dad's adjacent office was so quiet nowadays and mom dared not go in there in the evenings. It was a sacred place, but I missed the background noise of the adding machine or the *tap, tap, tap* on the computer keys. Sometimes I could forget he was dead and just imagine he was next door, working away, but the silence… always told the truth.

Kelsey plops down on my floor next to my desk and begins her story.

"Kate, I was riding to church tonight and Mrs. Potter started babbling about how much she loved church and how appreciative she is that I want to join them, blah, blah, blah. I almost checked out on it but then she starts talking about how when she drives to church she just knows the message of the day will speak to her. She went on to give all these examples of how she was struggling with her patience and then the pastor speaks about 'patience'. Or another time when she and Mr. Potter had a disagreement; the sermon that day was about 'forgiveness'. So now she just assumes the sermon will be exactly what she needs to hear."

Kelsey continues, "It reminds me of our clover tree and how we believe so strongly that it is true for us. Do you think church is Mrs. Potter's clover tree?"

I hadn't considered the clover tree in months.

CHAPTER TWENTY EIGHT

The first sign that something was wrong with my mom was her sleeping patterns. She has always been an "up and at 'em" type person; rousing us awake in the morning and proceeding to make our lunches while tuned in to the *Today* show. It has been our routine since we started Kindergarten. That doesn't happen anymore. In fact, it is rare that we even see her emerge from her bedroom before we go to school. It's not that we need her help to make breakfast and we've been buying lunch after all, we are both teenagers, but there is something very comforting about a loving sign-off from mom in the morning. I miss that. I miss her. I miss everything that changed when dad died.

These days I never know what to expect when I get home from school. But today, Kelsey and I agreed that it was a good day for both of us; a lot of distractions and upcoming events to look forward to. Kelsey has an art project that will be displayed in the lobby of the Seattle Art Museum amongst other young artists from local schools! It is a huge accomplishment and I am so grateful she is using her talents to direct her grief. We were celebrating her success as we walked in the house and hollered for mom. There was no response so we figured she was taking a nap or something. It was so unnerving having to track her down. It gave me flashbacks of entering the house the day dad died with the feeling of dread and despair. Why can't she be there for us? She wasn't in her room, yet the bed was messy—unmade, as if she had just gotten up or as if she was keeping it ready to get back in. Nevertheless, she isn't there so we keep searching and shouting for her. Even though it is raining heavily, we find her outside in the yard. Mom is drenched and oblivious to our presence. She is frenzied with a shovel and huge clippers. Hydrangea pieces are strewn all over the yard.

We yell loudly to get her attention, "Mom! Mom! What are you doing?"

In a voice mixed with anger and despair she answers back, "I am pulling out all of these stupid hydrangeas!" Kelsey and I walk down the stairs to face her.

Kelsey's eyes are brimming with tears. "You love your garden. Why are you destroying it?" she asks.

Mom doesn't stop digging as she replies, "I hate hydrangeas! I have always hated hydrangeas! Your father liked hydrangeas because they were his mom's favorite bush!"

I am in too much disbelief so Kelsey responds, "But Mom, then don't they remind you of dad?"

"Yes! And that is exactly why they are going! Everything reminds me of your father! I don't have a minute of solace in this house!" she shouts back.

I take Kelsey by the shoulders and lead her inside where we prop each other up and wrack ourselves with tears.

Mom continued her frenzy for another hour and then marched into the house. She went upstairs and slammed the door. We could hear her crying. When she came back down, she was dressed and showered.

"Kate," she said, "can you drop your sister off at soccer practice?"

"Yes," I quietly reply.

"And, pick her up?"

"Yes."

"Good." And then she opened up the fridge and poured

herself a glass of wine. That was yet another sign that something was wrong with my mother.

It seems the only thing we can do for mom is fend for ourselves and stay out of trouble. The pall of something greater than grief or sadness is upon us. Mom is totally unavailable and our house is no longer a safe haven for friends. I especially would never bring over a new friend; anyone who didn't know mom before dad died. She isn't the same at all and I never know what to expect. It is too embarrassing the way she either tries to be extra chummy to our friends or rants on about something stupid. On a good day, she'll mention what we are having for dinner. On a bad day, she'll be slumped on the couch zoning out in front of the TV. She is slipping away but Kelse and I are in survival mode with much more freedom and responsibility than we ever imagined.

At first, people were surprised to see us at the parties. The Malone girls, former rule followers and under the radar. But, as we frequented the parties, all of a sudden we have a new group of friends. We are actually curiosities to them and it is liberating. These people aren't afraid to just come out and ask, "So, you're the girl whose dad died in the freaky traffic accident, huh?"

"Yeah, that's me," I say as I pull from the keg.

"That sucks."

"Yep." So, it's not a therapy session but at least there are people who don't think I have a contagious disease. One of our first forays into the party scene is to Mandy's house. She greets me like we are best of friends.

"Hey, Kate! Welcome! Can't believe we haven't had a class together since LA in 9th grade! That's wild. Is this your sister?"

"Yeah, this is Kelsey."

"Hey, Kelsey. Have a good time."

"Uh, thanks," Kelsey's discomfort is obvious.

Mandy doesn't pick up on it, and adds, "I'll introduce you guys to some kids in a sec; I just have to find some more chips."

"That's cool," I say with some feigned confidence.

Admittedly, Kelsey and I are surprised by how many parents let their kids throw parties. But, I suppose, if we hosted a party these days, Mom may just jump right into the fun. As a bonus, boys I never even considered socializing with are becoming quite familiar and want to help Kelsey and me navigate the new scene. All this attention and new discoveries help me forget the new realities of my life. However, the introduction of partying has left less room for soccer and studies and red flags are being raised throughout our soccer families.

No one really knew what was happening at our house. Mom graciously takes a phone call or accepts a homemade meal from a concerned friend without letting on how she is coping with the grief. It's helpful that most people find it easier to avoid a sticky, uncomfortable situation because it enables the three of us to explore these new avenues undetected.

I make a bold move at lunch the next day and sit down at Mandy's table. I feel empowered and strangely confident amidst this alternative crew. I glance over to my regular spot and Madi is glaring at me and Morgan might be crying. Oddly, I don't feel bad about it; I'm entitled to have a different set of friends. I just don't see the big deal.

There's not a whole lot of difference in the flow of conversation. Dylan is telling a story about the substitute teacher in Math who couldn't get the class under control. Apparently, the ineptness of the teacher allowed Dylan to spend the entire period texting his buddies undetected. Then, Mandy starts talking about staying up until 1AM reading *Breaking Dawn* and Sam proposes that we sneak into multiple movies this weekend. I'm such a newbie that I may as well be invisible. Everyone is polite enough, but I honestly don't have much to offer so I finish my lunch and leave.

I'm intercepted by Madi. She's generally not confrontational but she's mad.

"Geez Kate. That was totally lame. Did you forget today is Morgan's birthday?"

"Oh crap," I mutter.

"Get it together Kate. I know you have gone through a lot lately but you can't keep hurting us."

The ice-cold demeanor of the new Kate responds, "Yeah, well, burying my father might not have been the rite of passage I was looking for this year."

"Dang it, Kate. We are so sad for you but you have to snap out of it. What would your dad think?"

"That's brutal Madi. Don't put that on me." I was so mad at the truth of it all that I went more sideways. "I'll make it up to Morgan. I'm outta here."

I sidle up to Mandy who fills me in on the big party at the lake tonight.

"It's going to be a throw down. A lot of kids; I think there might be some sporty kids too, you know, some of your old cohorts."

I laugh, "Cohorts." Great vocabulary word Mandy. "The party sounds rockin." That is exactly what I need to escape the attitude from my "cohorts".

Coach Tom reaches me on my cell after school. As soon as I realize who it is on the other end of the phone I reprimand myself thinking, you know better than to answer an unknown phone number Kate! It is a personal reminder about practice tonight-very unusual.

"Kate, remember I added a Friday night practice to get you guys ready for State Cup. Will I see you at practice tonight?" I am taken aback. I have been blowing off practices lately hence, the personal phone call.

"Ah yeah; I'll be there."

"Good. I really want you to demonstrate that you want to be on this team. As you've noticed, your playing time has already suffered. With your inconsistency and decreased effort, quite honestly Kate, your place on the team is in jeopardy."

I was so numb in general that his comment didn't have the impact it should have had, or would have had, a few months earlier.

"Got it," I answer without inflection. My lack of enthusiasm and borderline disrespect get his attention.

"Kate, you have played for me since U13. You have always been one of my most focused, disciplined and integral players. Do I need to talk to your mom about this?"

A quick inventory of my possible responses and I conclude that my mom did not need a call from my soccer coach. She has enough issues to contend with right now; namely, her own survival. So I added more enthusiasm and sincerity, "No, no Coach. That's okay. I will do better. Thanks for calling me!" I purposely don't fully commit to attending.

I'm not sure I was convincing but Coach Tom ends the conversation, "Okay, I will see you tonight!"

Mandy's text is too tempting, "RAGER AT THE LAKE. DON'T MISS IT. DON'T SHOW UP ON TIME. NO ONE DOES." I wish I could bring Madi or Sara but they'll be at soccer practice. I'm tired of them judging me anyway. Of course, Morgan isn't an option since she is mad at me. I need a wingman.

"Hey Kelsey," I probe.

"Yeah?"

"Do you have practice tonight?"

"Nope."

"Good. There is a party down at the lake tonight and I want you to come with me."

"Uh," she pauses, "can't you find someone else?"

"No, nobody else is available."

"Kate, I really don't want to go. It's all the older kids, huh?"

"Yeah, but they like you. I'll keep an eye on you and make sure you are having fun, okay? *Please.*" I know she wants to make me happy.

"We can't stay out too late," she insists.

"Deal."

"If mom even asks, tell her we are going to the mall."

She is torn and says, "But I hate lying to mom."

"She probably won't even ask. This way she won't worry." I'm attempting to sound like the voice of reason.

"She wouldn't let us go if she knew," Kelsey warns.

"Who knows what she would say. That was the old mom who cared where we went."

"Kate, that's not true. She cares. She's just sad."

"Sad. That's it." Kelsey is still too young to get it.

CHAPTER TWENTY NINE

This party is the antidote to my bad day. Screw Coach Tom, I'll deal with that later. Carpe diem! I throw my messenger bag filled with beer over my shoulder and head toward the masses. Kelsey reminds me, "Don't leave me, Kate."

"I won't," I say distractedly. I already see where I'm headed.

"Did you pack some Sprite?" she asks.

"I think there are a few in the car." I hand her the keys. "Go check."

"Wait for me," she pleads.

"I'll be right over there. I have my cell." I reach in the bag and pull out a beer. I crack it and work my way by various groups of people. I see some other younger siblings. Good, Kelsey can hang with them.

Mandy is the center of attention over in the picnic area. I boldly head in that direction. And then, in my line of sight, I see him. Totally out of context. Ryan.

"Your mom let you out of the house, huh?" I'm not pulling any punches. Ryan is part of my old life.

"I deserve that," he admits.

"Who you here with?" I ask.

"Nobody, I just thought I would check it out."

"Lots of kids showed up," I remark with little interest in the conversation.

"Yeah, they did. So, Kate, how are you doing?" he asks.

I hold up my beer as if to 'cheers' and say, "Fine, see you around." I feel so confused. Maybe it isn't Ryan who is out of context.

I feel Ryan's eyes watching me meander down the path toward the beach with Dylan. I don't get the sense that he is jealous. In fact, I break my cool and glance back only to see Devyn appear out of nowhere snuggling up to Ryan and whispering in his ear. Between the beer and Dylan's attention, her antics don't cause me much stir.

Holding Dylan's hand is invigorating and exciting. He is older and I feel thrilled that he noticed me. I want to walk slowly but Dylan seems impatient to get to the dock. It's a beautiful, crisp winter night and it feels like the whole school is here. But, I'm not mingling now; I find myself alone with Dylan Moore. He wastes no time and we are kissing at the end of the dock. It is almost surreal to me. Sometimes I barely recognize the Kate that finds herself partying at the beach. I'm engrossed, but my mind quickly flashes to my sister; I forgot to tell her where I was going. I hope she isn't looking for me right now. I better get back before she worries or gets herself into trouble. I pull away from his embrace and explain, "Dylan, I forgot to check in with my sister. She'll wonder where I am."

He leans in for another kiss, "She'll be fine."

"No, no. I better go." I'm dizzy from the beer.

He ignores my requests and begins to grope me. Nothing feels right about the firm hold he has on me. His right hand is on my butt and it's not an affectionate rub. He is using it to hold me tight.

"No, seriously. I have to get back to the party." I try to pull away but between his strength and my instability, I'm no match. My heart is racing and all my senses are in full alert. He reeks of alcohol himself.

"Kate, you are here now. Enjoy it." His left hand reaches for my breast.

I'm panicking. Again, I try to pull away from his arms but he continues.

"Dylan, really. I have to go!"

"No."

I'm in way over my head and scared. I make a final appeal. "Please. My sister will worry and maybe leave with someone else. I'm responsible for her."

"Kate, don't be stupid. I'll make sure everyone remembers what a prude you used to be if you leave now."

And then, I hear the equally panicked shrill of Kelsey, "Kate!" The interruption is enough for me to gain some wiggle room and I look over my shoulder. My sister, tears streaming down her face is galloping behind Ryan and they approach the dock heading toward us. Ryan looks furious.

"Kate, come with me. It's time to get you and Kelsey home."

Dylan pipes in, "Rescued by lacrosse boy; how lame." He pushes me toward Ryan and Kelsey, nearly tearing my sweater in the exchange.

We don't look back and continue up the path. At the top, I embrace Ryan and begin to sob. It's time to grieve properly.

I'm so ashamed. I gave myself and my sister a good scare tonight and all of Kelsey's fear from the scene was replaced by a manic need to unleash all of her worries. Conversely, I don't have much to say. All I know is that it's the first time in a long time that I feel taken care of. I feel the warmth of my dad's presence and protection as I sit next to Ryan. He is so good. I know I owe him an apology but I'm too exhausted and overwhelmed to address it now. I'll have to count on his continued forgiveness. He understands the rawness of my life. Something, I didn't even realize the magnitude of, until tonight.

Ryan walks us to the door to make sure we get in. I fixate on his eyes before I enter the house. I know he's mad. I was so irresponsible. But, I hope he sees all the gratitude and love I feel. We pause. Meekly, I thank him. And without a lot of confidence add, "Talk tomorrow?"

"Sure. Sleep well."

I walk in first. I'm so ready to go to bed. What a night. Kelsey and I don't even try to be quiet as it has been months since mom has worried about when we get home. I'll talk to Kelsey in the morning about what happened to me on the dock. It's time for me to make better decisions and help us find our joy again. My thoughts are interrupted by what I see outside our mud room entry. Mom moved our wingback chair into the space facing the mudroom. She looks so small with her knees against her chest and her face so sad and vulnerable. I am shocked that she is awake and monitoring our arrival.

I would normally be worried about our late arrival for fear of getting in trouble but since it has been so long since my mom has been the parent, I'm not worried. Instead, I feel parental, "Mom, what are you doing?"

Kelsey moves in behind me to hear mom respond in a barely audible voice, "Thank God you are home safely."

"Yes, we're fine. What's going on?" I ask.

"Girls, I'm exhausted. I'm dying from this grief. I'm jeopardizing everything with my denial. Tonight, I had a lucid thought and I panicked wondering where you were and what you were doing. And, worst of all, I was incapable of driving to find you."

After my own brush with vulnerability this evening I approach her. We embrace and tears punctuate a night of emotion. All I can muster are a few simple sentences, "Mom, I'm lost too. But, we are tough chicks. Let's get it together and make dad proud." Our bodies encircled, we made a silent pact.

The next morning, Kelsey and I are up first. I share with her my full experience on the dock. She shudders and admits that she hasn't felt comfortable in our new world of racy friends and parties. She wants to get back to her soccer friends and art classes. As I hear this

I feel so guilty that I pulled Kelsey into my own denial and negative behavior. I want to shake off the guilt, the grief, and the fog I've been in since my dad died. I flop down on my bed and cover my eyes. I start to cry. I cry and cry and cry. Kelsey rubs my back. When I am finished, my optimistic sister has a suggestion. "Hey, Kateet's invoke the clover tree together. Let's envision our life full of joy again. Okay?" I pull a clover off the tree and name it. We talk about what it would look and feel like to have joy again. Then, we close our eyes and complete the exercise with all of our senses and gratitude. It's our biggest wish yet for our generous clover tree.

Ryan calls first thing this morning to make sure we are okay. I agree to meet him at Starbucks later. But first I have some other important business to address. There are many broken fences, but I have to start somewhere.

I write them each a personal note in case I totally screw up the in-person apology. I add a bag of Skittles to the note because I need all the help I can get. Then I begin my pilgrimage of forgiveness late morning.

The waft of cooking bacon greets me first as I approach Morgan's front door. The comforting smell helps abate my jitters. Before I can even knock, her mom answers the door. Her smile and loving embrace nearly make me cry. I am praying hard that Morgan has an ounce of her mom's forgiveness in her.

I stammer, "Hi Mrs. Donaghue , sorry for dropping by unannounced but is Morgan here?"

"Yes, she is Kate. She will be happy to see you." I appreciate the helpful foreshadowing with her choice of words; it eases my anxiety. She adds, "Morgan is in the TV room. Go on in."

"Okay. Thanks." It's a long walk to the next room. I peer in. Morgan and her brother are watching TV. She looks up and sees me. I think her face lights up for a second before she remembers how much I let her down. "Hi Morgan."

"Hi," her blunt greeting reveals her pain.

"I brought you some Skittles… and a note. And, I want to take you shopping for a birthday present really soon…," I ramble on, "Morgan, I am so sorry about forgetting your birthday. I had an awful day yesterday for lots of reasons. One of the biggest was that I hurt your feelings. I'm so sorry." I would have kept talking but thankfully Morgan interjects, "Kate—it's okay. I accept your apology. You're my best friend. I just miss you."

"I know, I miss you too. I had to figure some things out but I'm okay now. So, you forgive me?" I ask.

"Of course I do. Maybe I haven't been supportive enough since your dad died. My mom and I were talking about it and maybe we didn't do enough for you and your mom and sister. We feel bad too."

"It's okay. No one knows what to do. I'm ready to move on in the right way; with you by my side?"

"Yeah, that's what I want too. Do you want to stay for brunch?"

"Gosh, I'd love to but I have a few more apology notes to drop off. I might sneak a piece of bacon on my way out though!"

"Kate thanks for coming by," Morgan says with all sincerity and wraps her arms around me in another loving gesture.

"No problem. Love ya" I squeak out before tears well up and I become a blubbering mess yet again.

"Love ya too!" Morgan assures me as I retreat down the path.

Lugging around a tail between your legs is exhausting. But, apology after apology goes well and my friends' forgiveness buoys me. Next stop, Starbucks to thank Ryan. I arrive first and order a few hot chocolates. He is right behind me. Ryan grabs a corner table and I join him.

"What a night," I offer. "Thanks for…," I start to say "the ride" but instead choose, "everything."

"No problem. I'm glad I was there."

"Me too."

"So, I don't know where you and I go from here but I wanted to say how sorry I am about your dad."

"Thanks. It's been awful."

"I bet. I went to the funeral."

"Yeah, I saw you."

"Your dad would have liked it a lot."

"It was nice. Mrs. Potter pretty much planned it."

"I liked the program. It's up in my room. It's a great picture of your dad."

"I think so too."

"My mom liked the flowers. There were so many!"

"That was my mom's…," I stop. "Your mom was there?"

"Yeah, sitting in the pew in front of me," Ryan replies.

"That was nice of her to come."

"She does like you Kate."

"She likes your agenda better." I smile but it still comes out snide. I want to take it back.

"True," he admits. It was nice of him to ignore the inflection. "I was wondering what you and Kelsey sprinkled over the top of the casket at the end of the service?"

"Clovers."

"Clovers? Because he's Irish?"

"Kind of, but not really. They represent something special he taught me and Kelsey."

"Oh, that's cool. You know, he taught me a lot too. We kind of stayed in touch."

"Really? He never mentioned it."

"Yeah, I asked him to write a letter of recommendation for me and we caught up every now and then." He continues, "Last time we talked he was asking me if lacrosse was my dream for myself or was it someone else's dream for me."

"He was like that. Real philosophical," I say.

"He wouldn't hang up until I answered and it was really hard to figure it out. Eventually I realized that it may have started out as my parents dream for me, but it morphed into my own dream for me."

"That's interesting. I have a question too. Even if the outcome is the same, you playing lacrosse in college. Do you think you would have taken a different path to get there had it been only your dream to realize?"

"Oh wow Kate. You sound like your dad."

"Thanks. But answer me," I insist with a smile.

He finally responds, "I definitely would have done it differently." He smiles. And, we both know what he means.

"So, that requires that I ask you this...."

"What?"

"What did Devyn think about you leaving her to rescue me last night?"

"You saw Devyn?"

"Yes, I'm that good." I smile wickedly.

"Kate, she told me to go help you."

"What?"

"Yeah."

"She saw you leave with Dylan and knows first hand what a creep he is. She insisted I go," Ryan explained.

"Wow."

"Yeah, I'm not sure I would've on my own. You looked like you were into it."

"I don't know what I was thinking." That's all I'm going to say about that; instead, I go back to the revelation. "I can't believe Devyn helped me like that."

"Even Queen Bee's can change," Ryan states.

"Yeah, I guess. I suppose it's my turn to be a good friend now," I admit.

"Maybe start with yourself, Kate. What are your next steps? Less partying?"

"Yes, I'm done with that. I need to get back into shape.

Hopefully, I haven't completely screwed up my chances on the Premier team."

"I have a feeling everything will be fine," Ryan assures me.

My journey of redemption continues toward the most unlikely place. With olive branch in hand, I approach Devyn's front door. It's a beautiful home and a massive door. It's as intimidating as the girl that lives behind it. To my surprise, she opens the door and says, "Hi Kate."

"Hi Devyn." We are both speechless, yet neither of us draws a weapon.

"You want to come in?"

"Uh, okay." I add, "I won't stay long. I just brought you something." I hand over the butterfly cage of Monarchs.

"What's this?"

"Don't you remember? Jr. High? Your tattoo?"

"Omigosh, Kate. Seriously?"

"Yeah, well. I just wanted to tell you something about the Monarch Butterfly. Even though its wings are as fragile as tissue paper, the Monarch Butterfly weathers terrible conditions to travel 2500 miles and manages to find its way home."

"Are you trying to tell me something Kate?" She smiles as she processes it all.

"Well, let's just say, you are stronger than you think. Thank you for standing up for me last night. I needed a friend and you were there to make sure I made it home."

"Wow Kate, you didn't need to bring me butterflies. But thanks. And, you really are too smart for your own good!"

"Alright, I'll take that as a compliment." I nudge forward to give her a hug. Devyn hesitates but accepts it. "Thanks again Devyn. See you around."

"Bye Kate. See ya."

Chapter Thirty

Nature is my church. It's not easy confronting grief but as I stride through the trails near my house, the thick skin of denial and anger is starting to peel away. I like running because the constant state of motion lets me cry in solace without making others feel uncomfortable. I like running because I can breathe deeply and make my lungs fill up with fresh air. I like the art of running because I can feel my strength coming back as my legs groan. I want my joy back and I feel like I'm on the right track.

Today I am running like a stallion. It's a clear winter day. The rains recently stopped and made way for a clear blue sky. My pace increases as I leave the pavement and hit the soil trails of the slough. I'm alone with my breath, the trail and my music. I know I should have more awareness of my surroundings but I'm enjoying how quickly time is passing in this state. Tears stream down my face and I don't even bother to wipe them off. It is so cathartic to release the pain this way. Images of dad flash into my head. He becomes alive in my mind as I put one foot in front of the other. My tears are the only indication that I know he is not physically with me anymore. It's comforting to have this time with him; yet, when the pace slacks and it's time to stop, I must let him go again.

I am running along peacefully but suddenly I have a strong

feeling to look over my left shoulder. I don't recall seeing anyone else on the trail, so I'm confused. Glancing over my shoulder I see a man on the bank of the slough waving his hands frantically! I stop, and my instinct tells me it is okay to turn back toward him. I take out my ear buds and try to understand what he's saying. I get closer.

The man points directly up and shouts, "Miss, Miss. Look over there! It's our lucky day!" I turn back around and look up. It's a cloud formation as vivid as those flowers that drape my clover tree. A clover shaped cloud hovering over my running trail. Its presence is not lost on me and I smile. Next, I turn back to thank the eager and enthusiastic stranger for pointing it out to me but he's gone. Was he even there? And, then, I look up even higher above the clouds and instead thank my dad for the message. "I love you Daddy!"

Driving home a text is coming through. I know I shouldn't look at it, but I do. It's Kelsey, "WHERE R U? DID U 4GET FAM DINR?"

Oh crap, I did. As part of our pact to "reclaim our lives" mom reinstituted family dinners. Starting tonight! This is so unsafe, but I text her back anyway, "B THERE IN 10. HELP ME OUT WITH MOM."

"K. HURRY!" Kelsey replies.

Did I even put the car in "park"? I run into the house as fast as I can. I feel terrible for disappointing mom. The savory smell of mom's homemade tomato soup is so comforting. I enter the kitchen to find mom and Kelsey giggling with each other at the table. They started without me, but I'm not feeling any tension about it.

"Hi Mom."

"Hi sweetie."

"I'm so sorry I'm late," I apologize profusely.

"No worries. I'm glad you are here. Kelsey was sharing with me a funny story about her wacky Science teacher. I think you had the same one, didn't you? Mr. Benson?"

As I served myself some soup, I answer, "Yeah, I had him in 7th grade." I lower myself into my seat and notice fresh flowers, placemats and linens. Mom really made an effort. I am grateful. "The table looks beautiful. I love the flowers."

"Thanks sweetie. I feel like flowers again."

There's camaraderie as we share our day with each other. I tell them about the cloud formation. They think it's cool too. Kelsey talks about the upcoming exhibit at the Seattle Art Museum. Mom encourages us to join her for her new, favorite workout: hot yoga. We express mild interest. Then she poses an idea about working at the local nursery. She thinks it will be a nurturing atmosphere for her and a chance to get away from the house and its memories once in a while. Watching my mother animated again as she discusses spring flowers is contagious. I look around and we are all smiling.

I raise my water glass to toast my mom and sister. They do the same. "The Irish are best when they have something to celebrate!" "Tonight we celebrate us—tough chicks," I proclaim.

"Tough chicks," they echo.

The painting took my breath away. Kelsey's humility is impressive as I take it in. I cannot believe what I see; in the foreground is a woman, very isolated. There is a sadness in her face but not morose. The wind pulls her hair backward and also rumples her dress. The paint melds a woman of great interest. She is lovely, calm and resigned. And then, the background comes to focus. It is blurry compared to the vision of the woman but I see it in all its clarity. In the background, are abundant clover trees; one by one they provide company to the woman who is finding herself both alone and lonely. Her hopes and dreams await her on the horizon. I consider it further as I stare at the canvas. So, she may be alone but perhaps she is not lonely. It is comforting and I get it. I reach over to Kelsey and wrap my arms around her shoulders.

"You understand it perfectly. Thank you for this."

She smiles back and says, "I love you Kate."

Entering the house is way less stressful now. I prefer my mom to be around when I get home but, it's not the unnerving event it was merely weeks ago. A box on the kitchen table catches my eye. There's a sticky note from dad's assistant that says: *"Here are the last few items from his desk. Fondly, Stephanie."*

Intrigued, I open the box. There isn't much inside. The first thing I see is the statue of St. Patrick. I remember it sitting on dad's desk. Then there is a pencil holder with pens and pencils. I wonder why they bothered to send this to us; weird. Also included is a can of unopened peanuts. Dad loved peanuts. I can imagine him sneaking handfuls throughout the day. And then, I see them. A collection of forgotten stories tightly rolled up, side by side. The calculator tape stories! But then, I think how dad was the last person to roll this up perfectly. Should I keep them intact or read them? I don't know what to do! My curiosity gets the best of me and I pull one from the pile randomly. I carefully unravel the paper and I take in a deep breath to recognize my dad's presence in this event. The first lines appear, "To Dad. Love, Kate- Ghost Story". It strikes me that I really don't remember writing this story. Somehow over the years, I convinced myself that I could recite those writings by heart but there is no recollection of this particular tale. And so, I read on, unveiling the imagination of ten year old Kate.

GHOST STORY

"Once **ther** was a **women.** Then the phone rang, she **answred** it and it said, I am the bloody **merdrer**. I am three blocks away. So she closed all her doors. It called again. It said I am two blocks away so she closed all her windows. It called again. It said I am one block away so she hid under her covers. It said I am at your bed stand, can I have a **bandade**?" By, Kate M

I giggle because it's pretty mediocre storytelling. There are so many spelling errors they seem to jump out at me on the page; and would you really call the person a murderer? And really, did I hear this on the playground and just write it down? Geez.

Then I'm wondering how it is that I cannot remember the content of the stories. Some ring a bell in my memory but for the most part, I would not be able to tell you what I wrote under dad's desk. If I cannot remember these, what else have I forgotten about my father? I start to panic at the idea, but I quickly determine that I'm in such a better place now. I take a deep breath and decide to talk to my dad directly through my thoughts. "Thank you for bringing this gift to me. I remember now. I remember our car ride together. I remember the maple bars. I remember the clovers….," I stop. That's enough. I grab the sculpture, stories and can of peanuts and take them up to my room.

CHAPTER THIRTY ONE

few months ago, their silence drove me away. But today, I welcome the silence. In my mind there is no more need to discuss the transgressions of the last few months: my irresponsibility, how I let my teammates down, how I let myself down. My dad, I'm sure, is not impressed. But, I'm trying to forgive myself since dad was always forgiving as long as we "Saw the lesson." So, I'm feeling like I can move on; especially, if everyone else can too. Yet, I'm nervous as I approach the field.

My nerves have no merit as Abbey runs up to me with a big hug. I could cry over the warm reception, again. I drop my bag and start warming up. My teammates couldn't be nicer and Coach Tom rounds us up. He starts with a joke like, "Long time no see," which isn't entirely funny but everyone laughs for some levity. I smile.

It's great to be playing again. I am strong, I am laughing, and I am feeling joy again. Kelsey was right, it *is* possible!

Practice ends and we break off to gather our bags and head home. I don't want this feeling to end. I feel loved, healthy and joyous for the first time in months. I want to stop time, wrap up this energy and carry it home with me.

Coach Tom approaches me as I'm packing up my bag. He is carrying a manila envelope. "Kate," he starts, "great practice tonight. It's super to have you back."

"Thanks," I reply. "It's awesome to be back."

He extends the envelope toward me. "This is for you."

I glance inside. It is full of cards and letters.

Coach explains, "We should have done this sooner. These are messages from your teammates and their families. We all loved your father a lot. We have been heartsick over the loss in our soccer family." He continues, "Kate, I'm sorry. Even adults don't always know how to handle these things, I mean, tragic events. We shouldn't have promoted silence; obviously it wasn't what you needed. Anyway, our hope is that these notes will provide you the strength and love to help you continue on your journey."

I am getting used to spontaneous tears so I don't feel self conscious when I throw my arms around him and lightly sob.

It is like Pandora's Box. I stare at the envelope knowing that while I would feel some comfort, the cards and notes would likely siege my heart and the pain would surface yet again.

So, I gingerly reach into the envelope and choose just one.

It was from Sara's mom. I couldn't have been more surprised at my reaction. I laughed and cried, wept and reflected. I held each one to my heart in an act of gratitude. These notes preserved memories of my dad:

"He was so kind to Madi after she left the team…."

"I will never forget the time he played a practical joke on me during our tournament in Oregon. I laughed so hard and it is my favorite memory from the trip."

"I didn't know your father well, but he was so generous and kind when you hosted our team party. I will never forget his genuine demeanor."

My heart is heavy over my loss; yet, light with the kindness of friends who could encapsulate their experience with my dad. Their memories gave his legacy more depth and meaning. What a wonderful gift!

I return the blessings back to the manila envelope but as I do, I feel something else wedged on the side. I reach my hand in for the last card, but it's not a card. I am not prepared to be staring back at the last family photo we have together. There he is—alive. Smiling right at me with his arm proudly wrapped around my shoulder. The stadium lights are on in the background and the four of us are so happy. I start to feel a bit nauseous, my grief starting to well up inside. I flash back to that evening of the High School Championship game. Dad was totally in his element watching me play and nervously joking with the other parents. I remember him predicting next year's line up with Kelsey on the field with me. He cheered me on and then picked me up after the loss. It's a joyful moment frozen in time. I stare at it realizing that dad will never get older but I will. As I do, I hope that this photo brings me comfort. I put it back in the envelope.

CHAPTER THIRTY TWO

I am feeling stronger. I am calling my new outlet for my grief "running therapy". When I run I feel spiritually, physically and emotionally strong. Knowing the girl I was before dad died, it is hard to believe I let myself drift so far off course. I was always so disciplined and reliable and yet, the tragedy shook me to the core. I realize now how much I relied on my dad's guidance. I mirrored his every encouragement and suggestion not wanting to ever disappoint him. When the reflection became my own, I didn't know what I was looking at and I ran away from it. Now, I run into it.

Running allows me to step out of denial and confront my pain and sorrow. With each stride and breath, I release some pain. Sometimes I must run farther or faster to feel relief, but I know that it is working. Mom suggests that I might be working my body too much and I hesitate to remind her that the alternative was quite a bit more destructive. What's more, my physical strength is parlaying into becoming a better soccer player. I missed soccer. I missed my friends. I have something I value so dearly back in my life. I visualize my newfound strength as I prepare for my soccer games. I relish in my new level of fitness as it allows me to focus on the plays and strategy. This new brand of confidence makes this part of my life… effortless.

I indulge my mother and join her for yoga. It's my attempt at solidarity and positive reinforcement for the progress she has made. I immediately question my decision as I gasp for air entering the hot yoga room.

Surprisingly, my soccer physique is not helping me out through this hot yoga class. The instructor verbally takes us into a position where my legs are three feet apart and I am supposed to straighten my legs, grab my ankles and touch my forehead to the floor. Yeah, right! My hamstrings are not budging and my breathing is labored! This athletic body is no match for the flexible ones flanking me in this class. Even my mother is having an easier experience than I am. Nevertheless, I try to quiet my mind, breathe and listen to the next instruction. I know a lot of time has gone by but this mental battle taking place on my particular yoga mat has no concept of time.

I am in a pose coined, "A human traction system," the instructor explains. I am balancing on my left leg that is as solid "As a tree trunk". Simultaneously, my left arm is lurching for the mirror and my right leg is being pulled up behind me with my right arm. My spine is bending like a taco into a position I'm sure it hasn't been in for awhile. All of that and keeping my balance is the challenge. It is taking all of my concentration to stay in the position and then the instructor says, "This represents the balance in your life. This is the balance of your life!" And I immediately tumble out of the posture.

The instructor takes us into "Balancing stick". As I lift my leg and press my arms toward the front mirror, all the while standing, I notice the tattoo on the shoulder of the girl in front of me. It's a yin/yang symbol. I wonder if Morgan and I should get one of those someday. As my mind briefly wanders, the posture ends. Everyone is standing tall looking forward. My goodness, the split second it took to form that thought was too long. This workout is intense. I take a deep breath and return my gaze to the front mirror.

Between the heat, the postures, and staring at my body in the mirror, I wonder which of these is the most challenging. The instructor insists we focus only on ourselves. I'm staring at Kate Malone in the mirror, all of me. I think to myself, wow, I think I seem taller. I feel very statuesque in this tree pose. The staring continues; hmmm, my normally straight hair is getting curly in this steam room. I kind of like it curly. When was the last time I actually looked at myself in the mirror? I stare into my eyes, what is behind there? Kate, what do you see? It turns out to be a rhetorical question. I don't have time to answer it right now anyway, the instructions keep coming. I feel like we are on the homestretch. I hope so.

I find myself in another awkward backbend posture. The instructor calls it "Camel". I am on my knees looking at myself in the mirror. I am instructed to put my hands on my hips, look back and move my hands down to grab my ankles. I am looking at the back wall. I'm uncomfortable but amazed to be in this position. It feels like an eternity as the instructor says, "Push your hips to the front mirror." And finally, she says, "Release." And that I do immediately. I pull myself up and feel a wave of nausea and dizziness. And then, I feel like I am going to burst into tears. I contain myself but it is difficult. My mom is looking at me like she knows exactly what is happening.

A few more postures and we are done. I am spent. I squeak out "Namaste" to the instructor as she leaves, echoing the rest of the class. I'm not sure there is enough water on the planet to abate my thirst at this point. In the locker room, the gals congratulate me. I do feel like I've accomplished more than just a workout. I'm wondering about the Camel pose. I ask my mom about my experience. "Mom, what happened to me after the Camel pose?"

"Well, sweetie, you opened your heart chakra and released some stored pain," she explains.

"Oh wow. That was weird. I thought I was going to cry."

"Oh, I know. When I first started practicing, I *did* cry after that pose. At first I was so self-conscious about it but then I realized that the atmosphere here is so full of love and forgiveness that I really never felt judged."

"You mean you burst into tears?" I ask.

"Yes, I did. It was like a reflex, spontaneous combustion or something. I could not control it or even anticipate it. It is a powerful posture for releasing emotional and physical toxins. Now, it is one of my favorite poses."

"That's good for you but I'm sticking with soccer!"

With State Cup on the horizon, school actually feels stress free. I once again find the lunch room chatter interesting. I do care about the latest Lululemon pants. What a relief. Madi's sleepover is coming up and I can't wait to spend a day with all my friends. I'm feeling whole again, like a piece of dried fruit immersed in water. I laugh at my analogy. I wonder if my mom would roll her eyes. I hope so!

CHAPTER THIRTY THREE

I didn't notice the Santa Clara coach talking to my mom. I was taking it all in during the awards ceremony. The "Dream Team", as we had been deemed at U13, was predominately intact and our grand finale was a State Cup victory. The hours of practice in rain, snow, intense heat and the sacrifices our families made to keep the commitment were enormous. I felt the same excitement as my teammates, but the hugs and high fives and the weight of the medal around my neck was only part of the victory. The victory represented a personal journey as well as a huge team accomplishment. My soccer family had lifted me up and given me the courage to reclaim a personal dream. I looked around and recognized that we had all been through so much in the last six months. I felt like a completely different person embracing the magnitude of it all; the victories along the way were not lost on me this time. I glanced up and mom was smiling ear to ear. Our eyes held mutual admiration and respect. "Tough chicks" we turned out to be—indeed.

Side by side my teammates and I pose for the Champions photo. We are giddy in the wake of our victory and we hold our medals proudly. Photos completed, we break up and mingle with friends and family. Amidst the crowd, the Santa Clara coach catches my eye and waves at me. How odd. As he heads in my direction, I stand still in anticipation. We had met before during high school soccer but that was before I nearly sabotaged my soccer career. Even so, he never gave me the impression that I'd have a place on his squad so I'm surprised to see him.

"Kate," he said. "Do you have a minute?"

"Ah yes, sure."

"Congratulations on the win."

"Thanks." I answer tentatively.

I asked your mom if I could speak with you. I have a few questions, is that okay?"

"Sure." The curiosity is killin' me.

"Kate, I have been watching you throughout the series. I've been really impressed with your performance; particularly, your focus and composure. What has taken you to the next level?"

My hand reaches for my brows and symbolically smooths down the right side as I take a few seconds to process his question. I haven't had to ponder such a question since my dad died. I take a honest stab at it. "Well, I've been on a personal journey and I had to remember a few things I had forgotten."

"That sounds interesting.. Can you elaborate?"

"I had to remember how to manifest my dreams," I explain.

"What do you mean?" he asks.

"Well, I've always worked hard to be fit and I'm innately competitive but the composure has come from a sense of knowing I have done everything I can to succeed and help my team succeed. I spend a lot of time visualizing the game and my performance. But, it is more than that; I can smell the pitch, feel the ball under my foot and the adrenaline of a perfect pass. I go over play after play in my head. I even visualized the awards ceremony that just finished. It becomes so real to me that I know there is no reason to feel nervous."

"That's fascinating and mature. Who taught you to do that?"

I pause; quickly look up toward the heavens and say, "My dad."

"You are lucky to have such an excellent mentor."

"Yes, I am."

Emerging from the crowd is a boy in a Notre Dame sweatshirt. He is heading straight towards me grinning broadly. Of course I know who it is. "Ryan! You were here! We did it!"

"You played great. Congratulations." He hugs me.

"Guess what? I did it too!" he exclaims as he points to his sweatshirt.

"No way!"

"Yes! I just got word last night; a full ride too."

"Your parents must be out of their minds."

"We all are."

"My dad would be psyched about Notre Dame. All that Irish pride."

"I know. We talked about it once when he was quizzing me about Division 1 schools. I would've sent him the most obnoxious sweatshirt I could find!" We laugh.

"And he would have worn it!" I say with confidence.

As we walk toward the parking lot, Ryan gets more serious. "Remember how I was telling you about some of the things your dad taught me?"

"Yeah."

"Well last night, after all the celebration over my scholarship, I started thinking about what it took to accomplish my goal."

"You've worked really hard Ryan," I say in agreement. "And made a lot of sacrifices," I add with a smile.

"I know; that's what I was thinking about. I'm super proud of myself but I had to ask, 'was it worth it?' "

"Was it?"

"Yeah, I think so. The reason I think I can say that is due to something your dad said to me once."

"Really? Do tell." I'll never tire of talking about my dad.

"He encouraged me to think of my lacrosse dream in terms of joy not obligation."

"Wow."

"There was a lot of obligation attached to that dream for a

long time. So, when I changed my thoughts about it, I could enjoy the journey; despite the sacrifices."

"That's awesome. You set yourself free."

"I guess I did," he acknowledges. "Kate, have you set yourself free?"

"I'm real close."

"I'm rootin' for you," he says.

"South Bend, Indiana is far away," I state.

"That's months away; Carpe diem, right?" he prods.

"Sounds good," I agree.

"Wanna go out to celebrate tonight?" he asks.

"I'd love to but my mom has something in mind. Maybe you could join us?"

"That'd be great." And, he slips his arm around my shoulders and ushers me toward my teammates. The familiarity feels good.

Still on a high from our win, I receive a phone call to catapult me into even greater joy. Mom hands me the phone. "Hello?"

"Hi Kate. It's Coach White from Santa Clara."

"Hi Coach." I have no idea why he is calling. I don't know what else to say.

"I'm calling because I have a proposition for you. I have been thinking about our conversation ever since I returned to California. I'd like you to come down and train with the team for a few days. I'd like to work with you on your ball skills. That's the easy part." He continues, "Your belief system, the visualizing, is more powerful than any skill set I have ever offered any of my players."

"Oh wow. That'd be great. Thanks." I am stunned.

"Super. I will make arrangements with your mom. One more question though. I did some research and learned that Olympic athletes use a similar technique to improve performance. Have you heard of that?"

"No," I replied. "The ritual just gives me confidence and a sense of knowing."

"Well, it's a concept I would like to incorporate into my coaching and quite frankly, my life. I'm impressed. I can't wait to learn more. See you soon!" He's ending the call.

The strong sense of knowing I just described envelopes me and I calmly reply, "Yep, see you soon."

I hang up the phone and collapse back onto my bed. How plans change. I recall some snippets of a conversation with my dad: "There are no guarantees. Even with a plan". And then there was something about architects and contractors and life not going smoothly. No kidding. With his words of wisdom resonating within me I decide I'm not giving up on Cal but sometimes the universe has plans that you should acknowledge and heed. Santa Clara might be the universe speaking. I will go find out.

The sun is peeking through my window illuminating my abundant clover tree. I lovingly glance over at my creation and think of my dad who gave me such a generous gift. I feel gratitude and love; the anger no longer lingering in my being. I forgive my dad for dying. And, I forgive myself. Then, without a prescribed thought about it, I find an unclaimed clover on my tree and label it, FORGIVENESS.

CHAPTER THIRTY FOUR

I open my eyes from a restful sleep to see my mother's smile. The joyful inflection in her voice is from what seemed, a distant past. Her eyes sparkle with excitement. Oh yeah, I thought in the haze of waking, today is the reception at the Seattle Art Museum for the Young Artists exhibit. Kelsey's painting has been on display all week. I remember that we are skipping school and as my mom put it, "So we can make a day of it." Mom prods me with her voice, "Kate, Kate. Time to get up sweetie! And, guess what? It's a day without rain!"

But I think, is it a day without rain or is it that the oppressive shroud of sadness has finally left us?

Kelsey sits shot gun as mom drives us into Seattle. I am in a good mood and feeling agreeable so I don't even utter a protest that I am older and more entitled to the front seat. But, after all, she is the guest of honor. Mom is right, it is a beautiful day. Mt. Rainier is to my left greeting us in all its glory. Now *that* looks like a painting.

I have the back seat to myself and the sunshine feels like a warm blanket. I'm relaxed so my mind wanders. I consider that a few months ago it is likely mom would have forgotten this reception entirely. Or, we wouldn't have even bothered to mention it. Those were dark days. I am so grateful for the rebirth of our family. My contemplative state ends when a text comes through. It's Morgan, "HEY, SOOOO MISSIN' U @ SCHOOL 2Y. C U AT RECEPTION LATR!"

"COOL. GLAD U RCOMING WITH UR MOM. IT MEANS A LOT 2 US," I reply immediately.

"NO PROB. PSYCHED 2 CKELS PAINTING. LATR!"

"LATR!"

I smile. Another thing for which to be grateful! We didn't get here alone. A lot of people held us in their prayers and positive thoughts.

It is more than its sheer size that causes it to eclipse the other paintings. The woman in the painting is mesmerizing. A small crowd surrounds Kelsey's creation. She's a curiosity to consider. Is she sad, peaceful, lonely, or contemplative? My intimacy with the subject matter allows me to know: it is all of the above. But, the group of admirers can come to their own conclusions.

Mom stops dead in her tracks. She doesn't need to ask which painting is Kelsey's. She swallows hard a few times and her eyes are welling up surely against all attempts to contain them. I know she doesn't want to make a scene but the grief, denial, and struggle of the last six months are culminating in this moment. It's almost too much for me to bear, watching her take it all in.

She approaches the painting without moving her eyes from the proud woman on the canvas. They are in silent communion with each other. Mom closes her eyes and puts her hand on her heart. Her other reaches up to join it. She squeaks out, "Kelsey, it is beautiful; absolutely beautiful." We all know that it is much more than "beautiful" but she is too awestruck to come up with anything else, I'm sure.

I chime in. "I know! Isn't it amazing? Inspiring!" I'm not doing much better with the adjectives but Kelsey witnesses how it affects us.

The three of us move away making room for more admirers to take it in. "I had no idea you could paint like that," mom admits. She is looking at Kelsey as if emerging from a coma. The obvious disconnect from the last few months is crashing in.

"I intended to paint something healing for us," Kelsey explains. "I spent weeks staring at the canvas until I remembered the clover tree. So, I visualized myself painting and it was always effortless. I even held my paint brush in my hand and waved it through the air, broad strokes, detailed strokes."

"Did you imagine that?" I point toward her canvas.

"No. The image I was painting was never perfectly clear in my minds eye. But even so, I felt confident I would be inspired if I could keep my grief at bay and tap into the feelings of joy."

There's that word again, "Joy". It seems to be inspiring amazing accomplishments.

"But, I was so sad it was really hard to get to a place where I felt healed and peaceful, not to mention joyous." Mom slips her arm around Kelsey as she continues, "That was an emotion buried deep. I almost tricked myself at first by remembering joyous events. As soon as I could reach that feeling, the brush took on a life of its own. This painting is what my feelings of joy and peace inspired."

My sister sounds so grown up. Just then an arm slips through the crook of my own arm; the Yin to my Yang.

"Morgan! You made it!"

"For sure. Hi Mrs. Malone. Hi Kelsey. I just heard from Sara. She's coming over with Madi and her mom."

"Cool. Thanks for coming."

"No prob. Hey, Kelsey, where is this painting anyway?"

"I will take you to it." And off they go.

I intended to go with them but I pause watching my friend and family walk away. I feel content. This is the feeling I imagined when I asked for joy back in my life. I wanted the angst and pain and bad feelings to go away. It's possible I will miss my dad every day of my life. At this point it's hard to know. But, I do know that I can replace the negative emotions with joy and peace. Today

I am surrounded by friends and family yet here I find myself standing alone. I catch a glimpse of myself in the bay of windows to my right. I can see clearly now who is in the reflection. I think it is even safe to say that the person looking back at me may very well be my best friend.

EPILOGUE

I can't remember the moment I realized that the power of the clover tree was actually within me all along. It was an evolution really; kind of like the weaning of a security blanket. You carry it and snuggle it long after you really need it; but somehow, its power stays intact. Perhaps it is the moment you no longer feel vulnerable or unconscious; that is the moment you can really trust yourself. And, ultimately love yourself. I still pick clovers in honor of my dad, his legacy, and my dreams.

ABOUT THE AUTHOR

Kimberly Foster earned degrees from UCLA and the University of Washington. Though, she admits, her formal education was no substitute for real life experience. As a mother of teenage girls, a proficient carpool "listener" and passionate storyteller, Kimberly offers her first Young Adult novel. She lives in Bellevue, WA.